Hail, Hail, the Gang's All Here!

Ed McBain was born in Manhattan, but fled to the Bronx at the age of twelve. He went through elementary and high school in the New York school system, and the Navy claimed him in 1944. When he returned two years later, he attended Hunter College. After a variety of jobs, he worked for a literary agent, where he learnt about plotting stories. When his agent-boss started selling them regularly to magazines, and sold a mystery novel and a juvenile science-fiction title as well, they both decided that it would be more profitable for him to stay at home and write full time.

Under his own name, Evan Hunter, he is the author of several novels, including *The Blackboard Jungle*, *The Paper Dragon*, and *Every Little Crook and Nanny*; as Ed McBain he has written the highly popular '87th Precinct' series of crime novels.

Also by
Ed McBain in Pan Books

Ed McBain

Hail, Hail, the Gang's All Here!

An 87th Precinct mystery

Pan Books London and Sydney

First published in Great Britain 1971 by Hamish Hamilton Ltd
This edition published 1973 by Pan Books Ltd,
Cavaye Place, London SW10 9PG
5th printing 1979
© Evan Hunter 1971
ISBN 0 330 23549 4
Set, printed and bound in Great Britain by
Cox & Wyman Ltd, London, Reading and Fakenham

This modest volume is dedicated to the Mystery Writers of America, who, if they do not award it the Edgar for the best *ten* mystery novels of the year, should have their collective mysterious heads examined.

(COERCION: A person who with a view to compel another person to do or to abstain from doing an act which such other person has a legal right to do or to abstain from doing wrongfully and unlawfully, is guilty of a misdemeanor. Section 530, New York State Penal Law.)

ONE

NIGHTSHADE

The morning hours of the night come imperceptibly here.

It is a minute before midnight on the peeling face of the hanging wall clock, and then it is midnight, and then the minute hand moves visibly and with a lurch into the new day. The morning hours have begun, but scarcely anyone has noticed. The stale coffee in soggy cardboard containers tastes the same as it did thirty seconds ago, the spastic rhythm of the clacking typewriters continues unabated, a drunk across the room shouts that the world is full of brutality, and cigarette smoke drifts up towards the face of the clock, where, unnoticed and unmourned, the old day has already been dead for two minutes. The telephone rings.

The men in this room are part of a tired routine, somewhat shabby about the edges, as faded and as gloomy as the room itself, with its cigarette-scarred desks and its smudged green walls. This could be the office of a failing insurance company were it not for the evidence of the holstered pistols hanging from belts on the backs of wooden chairs painted a darker green than the walls. The furniture is ancient, the typewriters are ancient, the building itself is ancient – which is perhaps only fitting since these men are involved in what is an ancient pursuit, a pursuit once considered honourable.

They are law enforcers. They are, in the words of the drunk, still hurling epithets from the grilled detention cage across the room, rotten prick cop bastards.

The telephone continues to ring.

The little girl lying in the alley behind the theatre was wearing a belted white trench coat wet with blood. There was blood on the floor of the alley, and blood on the metal fire door behind her and blood on her face and matted in her blonde hair, blood on her miniskirt and on the lavender tights she wore. A neon sign across the street stained the girl's ebbing life juices green and then orange, while from the open knife wound in her chest, the blood sprouted like some ghastly night flower, dark and rich, red, orange, green, pulsing in time to the neon flicker, a grotesque psychedelic light show, and then losing the rhythm, welling up with less force and power. She opened her mouth, she tried to speak, and the scream of an ambulance approaching the theatre seemed to come instead from her mouth on a fresh bubble of blood. The blood stopped, her life ended, the girl's eyes rolled back into her head. Detective Steve Carella turned away as the ambulance attendants rushed a stretcher into the alley. He told them the girl was already dead.

'We got here in seven minutes,' one of the attendants said.

'Nobody's blaming you,' Carella answered.

'This is Saturday night,' the attendant complained. 'Streets are full of traffic. Even *with* the damn siren.'

Carella walked to the unmarked sedan parked at the kerb. Detective Cotton Hawes, sitting behind the wheel, rolled down his frost-rimed window and said, 'How is she?'

'We've got a homicide,' Carella answered.

The boy was eighteen years old, and he had been picked up not ten minutes ago for breaking off car aerials. He had broken off twelve on the same street, strewing them behind him like a Johnny Appleseed planting radios; a cruising squad car had spotted him as he tried to twist off the aerial of a 1966 Cadillac. He was drunk or stoned or both, and when Sergeant Murchison at the muster desk asked him to read the Miranda-Escobedo warning signs on the walls, printed in both English and Spanish, he could read neither. The arresting patrolman took the boy to the squad-room upstairs, where Detective Bert Kling was talking to Hawes on the telephone. He signalled for the patrolman to wait with his prisoner on the bench outside the slatted wooden rail divider, and then buzzed Murchison at the desk downstairs.

'Dave,' he said, 'we've got a homicide in the alley of the Eleventh Street Theatre. You want to get it rolling?'

'Right,' Murchison said, and hung up.

Homicides are a common occurrence in this city, and each one is treated identically, the grisly horror of violent death reduced to routine by a police force that would otherwise be overwhelmed by statistics. At the muster desk switchboard downstairs, while upstairs Kling waved the patrolman and his prisoner into the squad-room, Sergeant Murchison first reported the murder to Captain Frick, who commanded the 87th Precinct, and then to Lieutenant Byrnes, who commanded the 87th Detective Squad. He then phoned Homicide, who in turn set in motion an escalating process of notification that spread cancerously to include the Police Laboratory, the Telegraph, Telephone and Teletype Bureau at Headquarters, the Medical Examiner, the District Attorney, the District Commander of the Detective Division, the Chief of Detectives, and finally the Police Commissioner himself. Someone had thoughtlessly robbed a young woman of her life, and now a lot of sleepy-eyed men were being shaken out of their beds on a cold October night.

Upstairs, the clock on the squad-room wall read 12.30 AM. The boy who had broken off twelve car aerials sat in a chair alongside Bert Kling's desk. Kling took one look at him and yelled to Miscolo in the Clerical Office to bring in a pot of strong coffee. Across the room, the drunk in the detention cage wanted to know where he was. In a little while, they would release him with a warning to try to stay sober till morning.

But the night was young.

They arrived alone or in pairs, blowing on their hands, shoulders hunched against the bitter cold, breaths pluming whitely from their lips. They marked the dead girl's position in the alleyway, they took her picture, they made drawings of the scene, they searched for the murder weapon and found none, and then they stood around speculating on sudden death. In this alleyway alongside a theatre, the policemen were the stars and the celebrities, and a curious crowd thronged the sidewalk where a barricade had already been set up, anxious for a glimpse of these men with their shields pinned to their overcoats – the identifying *Playbills* of law enforcement, without which you could not tell the civilians from the plain-clothes cops.

Monoghan and Monroe had arrived from Homicide, and they watched dispassionately now as the Assistant Medical Examiner fluttered around the dead girl. They were both wearing black overcoats, black mufflers, and black fedoras, both heavier men than Carella, who stood between them with the lean look of an overtrained athlete, a pained expression on his face.

'He done some job on her,' Monroe said.

'Son of a bitch,' Monoghan added.

'You identified her yet?'

'I'm waiting for the ME to get through,' Carella answered.

'Might help to know what she was doing here in the alley. What's that door there?' Monroe asked.

'Stage entrance.'

'Think she was in the show?'

'I don't know,' Carella said.

'Well, what the hell,' Monoghan said, 'they're finished with her pocketbook there, ain't they? Why don't you look through it? You finished with that pocketbook there?' he yelled to one of the lab technicians.

'Yeah, any time you want it,' the technician shouted back.

'Go on, Carella, take a look.'

The technician wiped the blood off the dead girl's bag, and handed it to Carella. Monoghan and Monroe crowded in on him as he twisted open the clasp.

'Bring it over to the light,' Monroe said.

The light, with a metal shade, hung over the stage door. So violently had the girl been stabbed that flecks of blood had even dotted the enamelled white underside of the shade. In her bag they found a driver's licence identifying her as Mercy Howell of 1113 Rutherford Avenue, age 24, height 5' 3", eyes blue. They found an Actors Equity card in her name, as well as credit cards for two of the city's largest department stores. They found an unopened packet of Virginia Slims, and a book of matches advertising an art course. They found a rat-tailed comb. They found seventeen dollars and forty-three cents in cash. They found a packet of Kleenex, and an appointment book. They found a ball-point pen with shreds of tobacco clinging to its tip, an eyelash curler, two subway tokens, and an advertisement for a see-through blouse, clipped from one of the local newspapers.

In the pocket of her trench coat, when the ME had finished with her and pronounced her dead from multiple stab wounds in the chest and throat, they found an unfired Browning .25 calibre automatic. They tagged the gun and the handbag, and they moved the girl out of the alleyway and into the waiting ambulance for removal to the morgue. There was now nothing left of Mercy Howell but a chalked outline of her body and a pool of her blood on the alley floor.

'You sober enough to understand me?' Kling asked the boy.

'I was never drunk to begin with,' the boy answered.

'Okay then, here we go,' Kling said. 'In keeping with the Supreme Court decision in *Miranda* v. *Arizona*, we are not permitted to ask you any questions until you are warned of your right to counsel and your privilege against self-incrimination.'

'What does that mean?' the boy asked. 'Self-incrimination?'

'I'm about to explain that to you now,' Kling said.

'This coffee stinks.'

'First, you have the right to remain silent if you so choose,'
Kling said. 'Do you understand that?'

'I understand it.'

'Second, you do not have to answer any police questions if
you don't want to. Do you understand that?'

'What the hell are you asking me if I understand for? Do I
look like a moron or something?'

'The law requires that I ask whether or not you understand these specific warnings. *Did* you understand what I
just said about not having to answer?...'

'Yeah, yeah, I understood.'

'All right. Third, if you *do* decide to answer any questions,
the answers may be used as evidence against you, do
you?...'

'What the hell did I do, break off a couple of car aerials?
Jesus!'

'Did you understand that?'

'I understood it.'

'You also have the right to consult with an attorney before
or during police questioning. If you do not have the money
to hire a lawyer, a lawyer will be appointed to consult with
you.'

Kling gave this warning straight-faced even though he
knew that under the Criminal Procedure Code of the city for
which he worked, a public defender could not be appointed
by the courts until the preliminary hearing. There was no
legal provision for the courts *or* the police to appoint counsel
during questioning, and there were certainly no police funds
set aside for the appointment of attorneys. In theory, a call
to the Legal Aid Society should have brought a lawyer up
there to the old squad-room within minutes, ready and eager
to offer counsel to any indigent person desiring it. But in
practice, if this boy sitting beside Kling told him in the next
three seconds that he was unable to pay for his own attorney

and would like one provided, Kling would not have known just what the hell to do – other than call off the questioning.

'I understand,' the boy said.

'You've signified that you understand all the warnings,' Kling said, 'and now I ask you whether you are willing to answer my questions without an attorney here to counsel you.'

'Go shit in your hat,' the boy said. 'I don't want to answer nothing.'

So that was that.

They booked him for Criminal Mischief, a Class-A Misdemeanour defined as intentional or reckless damage to the property of another person, and they took him downstairs to a holding cell, to await transportation to the Criminal Courts Building for arraignment.

The phone was ringing again, and a woman was waiting on the bench just outside the squad-room.

The watchman's booth was just inside the metal stage door. An electric clock on the wall behind the watchman's stool read 1.10 AM. The watchman was a man in his late seventies who did not at all mind being questioned by the police. He came on duty, he told them, at seven-thirty each night. The company call was for eight, and he was there at the stage door waiting to greet everybody as they arrived to get made up and in costume. Curtain went down at eleven-twenty, and usually most of the kids were out of the theatre by quarter to twelve or, latest, midnight. He stayed on till nine the next morning, when the theatre box office opened.

'Ain't much to do during the night except hang around and make sure nobody runs off with the scenery,' he said, and chuckled.

'Did you happen to notice what time Mercy Howell left the theatre?' Carella asked.

'She the one got killed?' the old man asked.

'Yes,' Hawes said. 'Mercy Howell. About this high, blonde hair, blue eyes.'

'They're *all* about that high, with blonde hair and blue eyes,' the old man said, and chuckled again. 'I don't know hardly none of them by name. Shows come and go, you know. Be a hell of a chore to have to remember all the kids who go in and out that door.'

'Do you sit here by the door all night?' Carella asked.

'Well, no, not all night. What I do is, I lock the door after everybody's out and then I check the lights, make sure just the work light's on. I won't touch the switchboard, not allowed to, but I can turn out lights in the lobby, for example, if somebody left them on, or down in the toilets, sometimes they leave lights on down in the toilets. Then I come back here to the booth, and read or listen to the radio. Along about two o'clock, I check the theatre again, make sure we ain't got no fires or nothing, and then I come back here and make the rounds again at four o'clock, and six o'clock, and again about eight. That's what I do.'

'You say you lock this door . . .'

'That's right.'

'Would you remember what time you locked it tonight?'

'Oh, must've been about ten minutes to twelve. Soon as I knew everybody was out.'

'How do you know when they're out?'

'I give a yell up the stairs there. You see those stairs there? They go up to the dressing-rooms. Dressing-rooms are all upstairs in this house. So I go to the steps, and I yell, "Locking up! Anybody here?" And if somebody yells back, I know somebody's here, and I say, "Let's shake it, honey," if it's a girl, and if it's a boy, I say, "Let's hurry it up, sonny."' The old man chuckled again. 'With *this* show, it's sometimes hard to tell which's the girls and which's the boys. I manage, though,' he said, and again chuckled.

'So you locked that door at ten minutes to twelve?'

'Right.'

'And everybody had left the theatre by that time?'

' 'Cept me, of course.'

'Did you look out into the alley before you locked the door?'

'Nope. Why should I do that?'

'Did you hear anything outside while you were locking the door?'

'Nope.'

'Or at anytime *before* you locked it?'

'Well, there's always noise outside when they're leaving, you know. They got friends waiting for them, or else they go home together, you know, there's always a lot of chatter when they go out.'

'But it was quiet when you locked the door.'

'Dead quiet,' the old man said.

The woman who took the chair beside Detective Meyer Meyer's desk was perhaps thirty-two years old, with long straight black hair trailing down her back, and wide brown eyes that were terrified. It was still October, and the colour of her tailored coat seemed suited to the season, a subtle tangerine with a small brown fur collar that echoed an outdoors trembling with the colours of autumn.

'I feel sort of silly about this,' she said, 'but my husband insisted that I come.'

'I see,' Meyer said.

'There are ghosts,' the woman said.

Across the room, Kling unlocked the door to the detention cage and said, 'Okay, pal, on your way. Try to stay sober till morning, huh?'

'It ain't one-thirty yet,' the man said, 'the night is young.' He stepped out of the cage, tipped his hat to Kling, and hurriedly left the squad-room.

Meyer looked at the woman sitting beside him, studying her with new interest because, to tell the truth, she had not seemed like a nut when she first walked into the squad-room. He had been a detective for more years than he chose to count, and in his time had met far too many nuts of every stripe and persuasion. But he had never met one as pretty as Adele Gorman with her well-tailored, fur-collared coat, and her Vassar voice and her skilfully applied eye make-up, lips bare of colour in her pale white face, pert and reasonably young and seemingly intelligent – but apparently a nut besides.

'In the house,' she said. 'Ghosts.'

'Where do you live, Mrs Gorman?' he asked. He had written her name on the pad in front of him, and now he watched her with his pencil poised and recalled the lady who had come into the squad-room only last month to report a gorilla peering into her bedroom from the fire escape outside. They had sent a patrolman over to make a routine check, and had even called the zoo and the circus (which was coincidentally in town, and which lent at least *some* measure of possibility to her claim) but there had been no ape on the fire escape, nor had any simians recently escaped from their cages. The lady came back the next day to report that her visiting gorilla had put in another appearance the night before, this time wearing a top hat and carrying a black cane with an ivory head. Meyer had assured her that he would have a platoon of cops watching her building that night, which seemed to calm her at least somewhat. He had then led her personally out of the squad-room and down the iron-runged steps, and through the high-ceilinged muster room, and past the hanging green globes on the front stoop, and onto the sidewalk outside the station house. Sergeant Murchison, at the muster desk, shook his head after the lady was gone, and muttered, 'More of them outside than in.'

Meyer watched Adele Gorman now, remembered what Murchison had said, and thought *Gorillas in September, ghosts in October*.

'We live in Smoke Rise,' she said. 'Actually, it's my father's house, but my husband and I are living there with him.'

'And the address?'

'374 MacArthur Lane. You take the first access road into Smoke Rise, about a mile and a half east of Silvermine Oval. The name on the mailbox is Van Houten. That's my father's name. Willem Van Houten.' She paused and studied him, as though expecting some reaction.

'Okay,' Meyer said, and ran a hand over his bald pate, and

looked up, and said. 'Now, you were saying, Mrs Gorman . . .'

'That we have ghosts.'

'Um-huh. What kind of ghosts?'

'Ghosts. Poltergeists. Shades. I don't know,' she said, and shrugged. 'What kind of ghosts *are* there?'

'Well, they're *your* ghosts, so suppose you tell me,' Meyer said.

The telephone on Kling's desk rang. He lifted the receiver and said, 'Eighty-seventh Squad, Detective Kling.'

'There are two of them,' Adele said.

'Male or female?'

'One of each.'

'Yeah,' Kling said into the telephone, 'go ahead.'

'How old would you say they were?'

'Centuries, I would guess.'

'No, I mean . . .'

'Oh, how old do they *look*? Well, the man . . .'

'You've *seen* them?'

'Oh, yes, many times.'

'Uh-huh,' Meyer said.

'I'll be right over,' Kling said into the telephone. 'You stay there.' He slammed down the receiver, opened his desk drawer, pulled out a holstered revolver, and hurriedly clipped it to his belt. 'Somebody threw a bomb into a storefront church. 1733 Culver Avenue. I'm heading over.'

'Right,' Meyer said. 'Get back to me.'

'We'll need a couple of meat wagons. The minister and two other people were killed, and it sounds as if there're a lot of injured.'

'Will you tell Dave?'

'On the way out,' Kling said, and was gone.

'Mrs Gorman,' Meyer said, 'as you can see, we're pretty busy here just now. I wonder if your ghosts can wait till morning.'

'No, they can't,' Adele said.

'Why not?'

'Because they appear precisely at two forty-five AM, and I want someone to see them.'

'Why don't you and your husband look at them?' Meyer said.

'You think I'm a nut, don't you?' Adele said.

'No, no, Mrs Gorman, not at all.'

'Oh yes, you do,' Adele said. 'I didn't believe in ghosts, either, until I saw these two.'

'Well, this is all very interesting, I assure you, Mrs Gorman, but really we do have our hands full right now, and I don't know what we can do about these ghosts of yours, even if we did come over to take a look at them.'

'They've been stealing things from us,' Adele said, and Meyer thought *Oh, we have got ourselves a prime lunatic this time.*

'What sort of things?'

'A diamond brooch that used to belong to my mother when she was alive. They stole that from my father's safe.'

'What else?'

'A pair of emerald earrings. They were in the safe, too.'

'When did these thefts occur?'

'Last month.'

'Isn't it possible the jewellery was mislaid some place?'

'You don't mislay a diamond brooch and a pair of emerald earrings that are locked inside a wall safe.'

'Did you report any of these thefts?'

'No.'

'Why not?'

'Because I knew you'd think I was crazy. Which is just what you're thinking right this minute.'

'No, Mrs Gorman, but I'm sure you can appreciate the fact that we, uh, can't go around arresting ghosts,' Meyer said, and tried to smile.

Adele Gorman did not smile back. 'Forget the ghosts,' she said. 'I was foolish to mention them, I should have known better.' She took a deep breath, looked him squarely in the eye, and said, 'I'm here to report the theft of a diamond brooch valued at six thousand dollars, and a pair of earrings worth thirty-five hundred dollars. Will you send a man to investigate tonight, or should I ask my father to contact your superior officer?'

'Your father? What he got to? . . .'

'My father is a retired Surrogate's Court judge,' Adele said.

'I see.'

'Yes, I hope you do.'

'What time did you say these ghosts arrive?' Meyer asked, and sighed heavily.

Between midnight and two o'clock, the city does not change very much. The theatres have all let out, and the average Saturday night revellers, good citizens from Bethtown or Calm's Point, Riverhead or Majesta, have come into the Isola streets again in search of a snack or a giggle before heading home to their separate beds. The city is an ants' nest of after-theatre eateries ranging from chic French cafés to pizzerias to luncheonettes to coffee shops to hot-dog stands to delicatessens, all of them packed to the ceilings because Saturday night is not only the loneliest night of the week, it is also the night to howl. And howl they do, these good burghers who have put in five long hard days of labour and who are anxious now to relax and enjoy themselves before Sunday arrives, bringing with it the attendant boredom of too damn much leisure time, anathema for the American male. The crowds shove and jostle their way along The Stem, moving in and out of bowling alleys, shooting galleries, penny arcades, strip joints, nightclubs, jazz emporiums, souvenir shops, lining the sidewalks outside plate-glass windows in which go-go girls gyrate, or watching with fascination as a roast beef slowly turns on a spit. Saturday night is a time for pleasure, and even the singles can find satisfaction, briefly courted by the sidewalk whores standing outside the shabby hotels in the side streets off The Stem, searching out homosexuals in gay bars on the city's notorious North Side or down in The Quarter, thumbing through dirty books in the myriad 'back magazine' shops, or slipping into darkened screening rooms to watch 16-mm films of girls taking off their clothes, good people all or most, with nothing more on their minds than a little fun, a little enjoyment of the short respite between Friday night at five and Monday morning at nine.

But along around 2 AM, the city begins to change.

The citizens have waited to get their cars out of parking garages (more damn garages than there are barbershops) or have staggered their way sleepily into subways to make the long trip back to the outlying sections, the furry toy dog won in the Pokerino palace clutched limply in arms that may or may not later succumb to less than ardent embraces, the laughter a bit thin, the voice a bit croaked, a college song being sung on a rattling subway car, but without much force or spirit, Saturday night has ended, it is really Sunday morning already, the morning hours are truly upon the city now, and the denizens appear.

The hookers brazenly approach any straying male, never mind the 'Want to have a good time, sweetheart?', never mind the euphemisms now. Now it's 'Want to fuck, honey?', yes or no, a quick sidewalk transaction and the attendant danger of later getting mugged and rolled or maybe killed by a pimp in a hotel room stinking of Lysol while your pants are draped over a wooden chair. The junkies are out in force, too, looking for cars foolishly left unlocked and parked on the streets, or – lacking such fortuitous circumstance – experienced enough to force the side vent with a screwdriver, hook the lock button with a wire hanger, and open the door that way. There are pushers peddling their dream stuff, from pot to hoss to speed, a nickel bag or a twenty-dollar deck; fences hawking their stolen goodies, anything from a transistor radio to a refrigerator, the biggest bargain basement in town; burglars jimmying windows or forcing doors with celluloid strip, this being an excellent hour to break into apartments, when the occupants are asleep and the street sounds are hushed. But worse than any of these people (for they are, after all, only citizens engaged in commerce of a sort) are the predators who roam the night in search of

trouble. In cruising wedges of three or four, sometimes high
but more often not, they look for victims – a taxicab driver
coming out of a cafeteria, an old woman poking around garbage cans for hidden treasures, a teenage couple necking in
a parked automobile, it doesn't matter. You can get killed in
this city at any time of the day or night, but your chances
for extinction are best after 2 AM because, paradoxically, the
night people take over in the morning. There are neighbour-
hoods that terrify even cops in this lunar landscape, and certain places they will not enter unless they have first checked
to see that there are two doors, one to get in by, and the
other to get out through, fast, should someone decide to
block the exit from behind.

The Painted Parasol was just such an establishment.

They had found in Mercy Howell's appointment book a
notation that read Harry, 2 AM, the Painted Parasol, and
since they knew this particular joint for exactly the kind of
hole it was, and since they wondered what connexion the
slain girl might have had with the various unappetizing
types who frequented the place from dusk till dawn, they
decided to hit it and find out. The front entrance opened on
a long flight of stairs that led down to the main room of
what was not a restaurant, and not a club, though it com-
bined features of both. It did not possess a liquor licence, and
so it served only coffee and sandwiches, but occasionally a
rock singer would plug in his amplifier and guitar and whack
out a few numbers for the patrons. The back door of the –
hangout? – opened onto a side-street alley. Hawes checked it
out, reported back to Carella, and they both made a mental
floor plan in case they needed it later.

Carella went down the long flight of steps first, Hawes immediately behind him. At the bottom of the stairway, they
moved through a beaded curtain and found themselves in a
large room overhung with an old Air Force parachute
painted in a wild psychedelic pattern. A counter upon which
rested a coffee urn and trays of sandwiches in Saran Wrap
was just opposite the hanging beaded curtain. To the left

and right of the counter were perhaps two dozen tables, all of them occupied. A waitress in a black leotard and black high-heeled patent leather pumps was swivelling among and around the tables, taking orders. There was a buzz of conversation in the room, hovering, captured in the folds of the brightly painted parachute. Behind the counter, a man in a white apron was drawing a cup of coffee from the huge silver urn. Carella and Hawes walked over to him. Carella was almost six feet tall, and he weighed a hundred and eighty pounds, with wide shoulders and a narrow waist and the hands of a street brawler. Hawes was six feet two inches tall, and he weighed a hundred and ninety-five pounds bone-dry, and his hair was a fiery red with a white streak over the left temple, where he had once been knifed while investigating a burglary. Both men looked like exactly what they were: fuzz.

'What's the trouble?' the man behind the counter asked immediately.

'No trouble,' Carella said. 'This your place?'

'Yes. My name is Georgie Bright, and I already been visited, thanks. Twice.'

'Oh? Who visited you?'

'First time a cop named O'Brien, second time a cop named Parker. I already cleared up that whole thing that was going on downstairs.'

'What whole thing going on downstairs?'

'In the men's room. Some kids were selling pot down there, it got to be a regular neighbourhood supermarket. So I done what O'Brien suggested, I put a man down there outside the toilet door, and the rule now is only one person goes in there at a time. Parker came around to make sure I was keeping my part of the bargain. I don't want no narcotics trouble here. Go down and take a look if you like. You'll see I got a man watching the toilet.'

'Who's watching the man watching the toilet?' Carella asked.

'That ain't funny,' Georgie Bright said, looking offended.

'Know anybody named Harry?' Hawes asked.

'Harry who? I know a lot of Harrys.'

'Any of them here tonight?'

'Maybe.'

'Where?'

'There's one over there near the bandstand. The big guy with the blond hair.'

'Harry what?'

'Donatello.'

'Make the name?' Carella asked Hawes.

'No,' Hawes said.

'Neither do I.'

'Let's talk to him.'

'You want a cup of coffee or something?' Georgie Bright asked.

'Yeah, why don't you send some over to the table?' Hawes said, and followed Carella across the room to where Harry Donatello was sitting with another man. Donatello was wearing grey slacks, black shoes and socks, a white shirt open at the throat, and a double-breasted blue blazer. His long blond hair was combed straight back from the forehead, revealing a sharply defined widow's peak. He was easily as big as Hawes, and he sat with his hands folded on the table in front of him, talking to the man who sat opposite him. He did not look up as the detectives approached.

'Is your name Harry Donatello?' Carella asked.

'Who wants to know?'

'Police officers,' Carella said, and flashed his shield.

'I'm Harry Donatello, what's the matter?'

'Mind if we sit down?' Hawes asked, and before Donatello could answer, both men sat, their backs to the empty bandstand and the exit door.

'Do you know a girl named Mercy Howell?' Carella asked.

'What about her?'

'Do you know her?'

'I know her. What's the beef? She under age or something?'

'When did you see her last?'

The man with Donatello, who up to now had been silent, suddenly piped, 'You don't have to answer no questions without a lawyer, Harry. Tell them you want a lawyer.'

The detectives looked him over. He was small and thin, with black hair combed sideways to conceal a receding hairline. He was badly in need of a shave. He was wearing blue trousers and a striped shirt.

'This is a field investigation,' Hawes said dryly, 'and we can ask anything we damn please.'

'Town's getting full of lawyers,' Carella said. 'What's your name, counsellor?'

'Jerry Riggs. You going to drag *me* in this, whatever it is?'

'It's a few friendly questions in the middle of the night,' Hawes said. 'Anybody got any objections to that?'

'Getting so two guys can't even sit and talk together without getting shook down,' Riggs said.

'You've got a tough life, all right,' Hawes said, and the girl in the black leotard brought their coffee to the table, and then hurried off to take another order. Donatello watched her jiggling behind as she swivelled across the room.

'So when's the last time you saw the Howell girl?' Carella asked again.

'Wednesday night,' Donatello said.

'Did you see her tonight?'

'No.'

'Were you *supposed* to see her tonight?'

'Where'd you get that idea?'

'We're full of ideas,' Hawes said.

'Yeah, I was supposed to meet her here ten minutes ago. Dumb broad is late, as usual.'

'What do you do for a living, Donatello?'

'I'm an importer. You want to see my business card?'

'What do you import?'

'Souvenir ashtrays.'

'How'd you get to know Mercy Howell?'

'I met her at a party in The Quarter. She got a little high, and she done her thing.'

'What thing?'

'The thing she does in that show she's in.'

'Which is what?'

'She done this dance where she takes off all her clothes.'

'How long have you been seeing her?'

'I met her a couple of months ago. I see her on and off, maybe once a week, something like that. This town is full of broads, you know, a guy don't have to get himself involved in no relationship with no specific broad.'

'What was your relationship with *this* specific broad?'

'We have a few laughs together, that's all. She's a swinger, little Mercy,' Donatello said, and grinned at Riggs.

'Want to tell us where you were tonight between eleven and twelve?'

'Is this still a *field* investigation?' Riggs asked sarcastically.

'Nobody's in custody yet,' Hawes said, 'so let's cut the legal crap, okay? Tell us where you were, Donatello.'

'Right here,' Donatello said. 'From ten o'clock till now.'

'I suppose somebody saw you here during that time.'

'A *hundred* people saw me.'

A crowd of angry black men and women were standing outside the shattered window of the storefront church. Two fire engines and an ambulance were parked at the kerb. Kling pulled in behind the second engine, some ten feet away from the hydrant. It was almost 2.30 AM on a bitterly cold October night, but the crowd looked and sounded like a mob at an afternoon street-corner rally in the middle of August. Restless, noisy, abrasive, anticipative, they ignored the penetrating cold and concentrated instead on the burning issue of the hour, the fact that a person or persons unknown had thrown a bomb through the plate-glass window of the church. The beat patrolman, a newly appointed cop who felt vaguely uneasy in this neighbourhood even during his daytime shift, greeted Kling effusively, his pale white face bracketed by ear-muffs, his gloved hands clinging desperately to his nightstick. The crowd parted to let Kling through. It did not help that he was the youngest man on the squad, with the callow look of a country bumpkin on his unlined face, it did not help that he was blond and hatless, it did not help that he walked into the church with the confident stride of a champion come to set things right. The crowd knew he was fuzz, and they knew he was Whitey, and they knew, too, that if this bombing had taken place on Hall Avenue crosstown and downtown, the Police Commissioner himself would have arrived behind a herald of official trumpets. This, however, was Culver Avenue, where a boiling mixture of Puerto Ricans, and Negroes shared a disintegrating ghetto, and so the car that pulled to the kerb was not marked with the Commissioner's distinctive blue-and-gold seal, but was instead a green Chevy convertible that belonged to Kling himself, and the man who stepped out of it looked young and inexperienced and inept despite the confident stride he affected as he walked into the church, his shield pinned to his overcoat.

The bomb had caused little fire damage, and the firemen already had the flames under control, their hoses snaking through and around the overturned folding chairs scattered about the small room. Ambulance attendants picked their way over the hoses and around the debris, carrying out the injured – the dead could wait.

'Have you called the Bomb Squad?' Kling asked the patrolman.

'No,' the patrolman answered, shaken by the sudden possibility that he had been derelict in his duty.

'Why don't you do that now?' Kling suggested.

'Yes, *sir*,' the patrolman answered, and rushed out. The ambulance attendants went by with a moaning woman on a stretcher. She was still wearing her eyeglasses, but one lens had been shattered and blood was running in a steady rivulet down the side of her nose. The place stank of gunpowder and smoke and charred wood. The most serious damage had been done at the rear of the small store, farthest away from the entrance door. Whoever had thrown the bomb must have possessed a damn good pitching arm to have hurled it so accurately through the window and across the fifteen feet to the makeshift altar. The minister lay across his own altar, dead, one arm blown off in the explosion. Two women who had been sitting on folding chairs closest to the altar lay upon each other on the floor now, tangled in death, their clothes still smouldering. The sounds of the injured filled the room, and then were suffocated by the overriding siren-shriek of the arriving second ambulance. Kling went outside to the crowd.

'Anybody here witness this?' he asked.

A young man, black, wearing a beard and a natural hair style, turned away from a group of other youths, and walked directly to Kling.

'Is the minister dead?' he asked.

'Yes, he is,' Kling answered.

'Who else?'

'Two women.'

'Who?'

'I don't know yet. We'll identify them as soon as the men are through in there.' He turned again to the crowd. 'Did anybody see what happened?' he asked.

'I saw it,' the young man said.

'What's your name, son?'

'Andrew Jordan.'

Kling took out his pad. 'All right, let's have it.'

'What good's this going to do?' Jordan asked. 'Writing all this shit in your book?'

'You said you saw what . . .'

'I saw it, all right. I was walking by, heading for the poolroom up the street, and the ladies were inside singing, and this car pulled up, and a guy got out, threw the bomb, and ran back to the car.'

'What kind of a car was it?'

'A red VW.'

'What year?'

'Who can tell with those VWs?'

'How many people in it?'

'Two. The driver and the guy who threw the bomb.'

'Notice the licence plate?'

'No. They drove off too fast.'

'Can you describe the man who threw the bomb?'

'Yeah. He was white.'

'What else?' Kling asked.

'That's all,' Jordan replied. 'He was *white*.'

There were perhaps three dozen estates in all of Smoke Rise, a hundred or so people living in luxurious near seclusion on acres of valuable land through which ran four winding, interconnected, private roadways. Meyer Meyer drove between the wide stone pillars marking Smoke Rise's western access road, entering a city within a city, bounded on the north by the River Harb, shielded from the River Highway by stands of poplars and evergreens on the south – exclusive Smoke Rise, known familiarly and derisively to the rest of the city's inhabitants as 'The Club'.

374 MacArthur Lane was at the end of the road that curved past the Hamilton Bridge. The house was a huge grey stone structure with a slate roof and scores of gables and chimneys jostling the sky, perched high in gloomy shadow above the Harb. As he stepped from the car, Meyer could hear the sounds of river traffic, the hooting of tugs, the blowing of whistles, the eruption of a squawk box on a destroyer midstream. He looked out over the water. Reflected lights glistened in shimmering liquid beauty, the hanging globes on the bridge's suspension cables, the dazzling reds and greens of signal lights on the opposite shore, single illuminated window slashes in apartment buildings throwing their mirror images onto the black surface of the river, the blinking wing lights of an aeroplane overhead moving in watery reflection like a submarine. The air was cold, a fine piercing drizzle had begun several minutes ago. Meyer shuddered, pulled the collar of his coat higher on his neck, and walked towards the old grey house, his shoes crunching on the driveway gravel, the sound echoing away into the high surrounding bushes.

The stones of the old house oozed wetness. Thick vines

covered the walls, climbing to the gabled, turreted roof. He found a doorbell set over a brass escutcheon in the thick oaken doorjamb, and pressed it. Chimes sounded somewhere deep inside the house. He waited.

The door opened suddenly.

The man looking out at him was perhaps seventy years old, with piercing blue eyes, bald except for white thatches of hair that sprang wildly from behind each ear. He wore a red smoking jacket and black trousers, a black ascot around his neck, red velvet slippers.

'What do you want?' he asked immediately.

'I'm Detective Meyer of the Eighty-seventh . . .'

'Who sent for you?'

'A woman named Adele Gorman came to the . . .'

'My daughter's a fool,' the man said. 'We don't need the police here,' and slammed the door in his face.

Meyer stood on the doorstep feeling somewhat like a horse's ass. A tugboat hooted on the river. A light snapped on upstairs, casting at the luminous dial of his watch. It was 2.35 AM. The drizzle was cold and penetrating. He took out his handkerchief, blew his nose, and wondered what he should do next. He did not like ghosts, and he did not like lunatics, and he did not like nasty old men who did not comb their hair and who slammed doors in a person's face. He was about to head back for his car when the door opened again.

'Detective Meyer?' Adele Gorman said. 'Do come in.'

'Thank you,' he said, and stepped into the entrance foyer.

'You're right on time.'

'Well, a little early actually,' Meyer said. He still felt foolish. What the hell was he doing in Smoke Rise investigating ghosts in the middle of the night?

'This way,' Adele said, and he followed her through a sombrely panelled foyer into a vast, dimly lighted living-room. Heavy oaken beams ran overhead, velvet curtains hung at the window, the room was cluttered with ponderous old furniture. He could believe there were ghosts in this house, he could suddenly believe it. A young man wearing dark glasses rose like a spectre from the sofa near the fireplace. His face, illuminated by the single standing floor lamp, looked wan and drawn. Wearing a black cardigan sweater over a white shirt and dark slacks, he approached Meyer unsmilingly with his hand extended – but he did not accept Meyer's hand when it was offered in return.

Meyer suddenly realized that the man was blind.

'I'm Ralph Gorman,' he said, his hand still extended. 'Adele's husband.'

'How do you do, Mr. Gorman,' Meyer said, and took his hand. The palm was moist and cold.

'It was good of you to come,' Gorman said. 'These apparitions have been driving us crazy.'

'What time is it?' Adele asked suddenly, and looked at her watch. 'We've got five minutes,' she said. There was a tremor in her voice. She seemed suddenly very frightened.

'Won't your father be here?' Meyer asked.

'No, he's gone up to bed,' Adele said. 'I'm afraid he's bored with the whole affair, and terribly angry that we notified the police.'

Meyer made no comment. Had he known that Willem Van Houten, former Surrogate's Court judge, had *not* wanted the police to be notified, Meyer would not have been here in the first place. He debated leaving now, but Adele Gorman had begun talking again, and it was impolite to depart in the middle of another person's sentence.

'. . . is in her early thirties, I would guess. The other ghost, the male, is about your age – forty or forty-five, something like that.'

'I'm thirty-seven,' Meyer said.

'Oh.'

'The bald head fools a lot of people.'

'Yes.'

'I was bald at a very early eage.'

'Anyway,' Adele said, 'their names are Elisabeth and Johann, and they've probably been . . .'

'Oh, they have names, do they?'

'Yes. They're ancestors, you know. My father is Dutch, and there actually *were* an Elisabeth and Johann Van Houten in the family centuries ago, when Smoke Rise was still a Dutch settlement.'

'They're Dutch, um-huh, I see,' Meyer said.

'Yes. They always appear wearing Dutch costumes. And they also speak Dutch.'

'Have *you* heard them, Mr Gorman?'

'Yes,' Gorman said. 'I'm blind, you know . . .' he added, and hesitated, as though expecting some comment from Meyer. When none came, he said, 'But I *have* heard them.'

'Do you speak Dutch?'

'No. My father-in-law speaks it fluently, though, and he identified the language for us, and told us what they were saying.'

'What *did* they say?'

'Well, for one thing, they said they were going to steal Adele's jewellery, and they damn well did.'

'Your *wife's* jewellery? But I thought . . .'

'It was willed to her by her mother. My father-in-law keeps it in his safe.'

'*Kept*, you mean.'

'No, keeps. There are several pieces in addition to the ones that were stolen. Two rings and also a necklace.'

'And the value?'

'All together? I would say about forty thousand dollars.'

'Your ghosts have expensive taste.'

The floor lamp in the room suddenly began to flicker. Meyer glanced at it and felt the hackles rising at the back of his neck.

'The lights are going out, Ralph,' Adele whispered.

'Is it two forty-five?'

'Yes.'

'They're here,' Gorman whispered.

Mercy Howell's roommate had been asleep for close to four hours when they knocked on her door. But she was a wily young lady, hip to the ways of the big city, and very much awake as she conducted her own little investigation without so much as opening the door a crack. First she asked them to spell their names slowly. Then she asked them their shield numbers. Then she asked them to hold their shields and their ID cards close to the door's peephole, where she could see them. Still unconvinced, she said through the locked door, 'You just wait there a minute.' They waited for close to five minutes before they heard her approaching the door again. The heavy steel bar of a Fox lock was pushed noisily to the side, a safety chain rattled on its track, the tumblers of one lock clicked open, and then another, and finally the girl opened the door.

'Come in,' she said, 'I'm sorry I kept you waiting. I called the station house and they said you were okay.'

'You're a very careful girl,' Hawes said.

'At this hour of the morning? Are you kidding?' she said.

She was perhaps twenty-five, with her red hair up in curlers, her face cold-creamed clean of makeup. She was wearing a pink quilted robe over flannel pyjamas, and although she was probably a very pretty girl at 9 AM, she now looked about as attractive as a Buffalo nickel.

'What's your name, miss?' Carella asked.

'Lois Kaplan. What's all this about? Has there been another burglary in the building?'

'No, Miss Kaplan. We want to ask you some questions about Mercy Howell. Did she live here with you?'

'Yes,' Lois said, and suddenly looked at them shrewdly. 'What do you mean *did*? She still *does*.'

They were standing in the small foyer of the apartment, and the foyer went so still that all the night sounds of the building were clearly audible all at once, as though they had not been there before but had only been summoned up now to fill the void of silence. A toilet flushed somewhere, a hot water pipe rattled, a baby whimpered, a dog barked, someone dropped a shoe. In the foyer now filled with noise, they stared at each other wordlessly, and finally Carella drew a deep breath and said, 'Your roommate is dead. She was stabbed tonight as she was leaving the theatre.'

'No,' Lois said, simply and flatly and unequivocally. 'No, she isn't.'

'Miss Kaplan . . .'

'I don't give a damn what you say, Mercy isn't dead.'

'Miss Kaplan, she's dead.'

'Oh Jesus,' Lois said, and burst into tears, 'oh Jesus, oh damn damn, oh Jesus.'

The two men stood by feeling stupid and big and awkward and helpless. Lois Kaplan covered her face with her hands and sobbed into them, her shoulders heaving, saying over and over again, 'I'm sorry, oh Jesus, please, I'm sorry, please, oh poor Mercy, oh my God,' while the detectives tried not to watch. At last the crying stopped and she looked up at them with eyes that had been knifed, and said softly, 'Come in. Please,' and led them into the living-room. She kept staring at the floor as she talked. It was as if she could not look them in the face, not these men who had brought her the news.

'Do you know who did it?' she asked.

'No. Not yet.'

'We wouldn't have waked you in the middle of the night . . .'

'That's all right.'

'But very often, if we get moving on a case fast enough, before the trail gets cold . . .'

'Yes, I understand.'

'We can often . . .'

'Yes, before the the trail gets cold,' Lois said.

'Yes.'

The apartment went silent again.

'Would you know if Miss Howell had any enemies?' Carella asked.

'She was the sweetest girl in the world,' Lois said.

'Did she argue with anyone recently, were there? . . .'

'No.'

'. . . any threatening telephone calls or letters?'

Lois Kaplan looked up at them.

'Yes,' she said. 'A letter.'

'A *threatening* letter?'

'We couldn't tell. It frightened Mercy, though. That's why she bought the gun.'

'What kind of gun?'

'I don't know. A small one.'

'Would it have been a .25 calibre Browning?'

'I don't know guns.'

'Was this letter mailed to her, or delivered personally?'

'It was mailed to her. At the theatre.'

'When?'

'A week ago.'

'Did she report it to the police?'

'No.'

'Why not?'

'Haven't you seen *Rattlesnake*?' Lois said.

'What do you mean?' Carella said.

'*Rattlesnake*. The musical. Mercy's show. The show she was in.'

'No, I haven't.'

'But you've *heard* of it.'

'No.'

'Where do you live, for God's sake? On the moon?'

'I'm sorry, I just haven't . . .'

'Forgive me,' Lois said immediately. 'I'm not usually . . . I'm trying very hard to . . . I'm sorry. Forgive me.'

'That's all right,' Carella said.

'Anyway, it's . . . it's a big hit now but . . . there was trouble in the beginning, you see . . . are you *sure* you don't know about this? It was in all the newspapers.'

'Well, I guess I missed it,' Carella said. 'What was the trouble about?'

'Don't *you* know about this either?' she asked Hawes.

'No, I'm sorry.'

'About Mercy's dance?'

'No.'

'Well, in one scene, Mercy danced the title song without any clothes on. Because the idea was to express . . . the *hell* with what the idea was. The point is that the dance wasn't at all prurient, it wasn't even sexy! But the police *missed* the point, and closed the show down two days after it opened. The producers had to go to court for a writ to get the show opened again.'

'Yes, I remember it now,' Carella said.

'What I'm trying to say is that nobody involved with *Rattlesnake* would report *anything* to the police. Not even a threatening letter.'

'If she bought a pistol,' Hawes said, 'she would have *had* to go to the police. For a permit.'

'She didn't have a permit.'

'Then how'd she get the pistol? You can't buy a handgun without first . . .'

'A friend of hers sold it to her.'

'What's the friend's name?'

'Harry Donatello.'

'An importer,' Carella said dryly.

'Of souvenir ashtrays,' Hawes said.

'I don't know what he does for a living,' Lois said. 'But he got the gun for her.'

'When was this?'

'A few days after she received the letter.'

'What did the letter say?' Carella asked.

'I'll get it for you,' Lois said, and went into the bedroom. They heard a dresser drawer opening, the rustle of clothes, what might have been a tin candy box being opened. Lois came back into the room. 'Here it is,' she said.

There didn't seem much point in trying to preserve latent prints on a letter that had already been handled by Mercy Howell, Lois Kaplan, and God knew how many others. But Carella none the less accepted the letter on a handkerchief spread over the palm of his hand, and then looked at the face of the envelope. 'She should have brought this to us immediately,' he said. 'It's written on hotel stationery, we've got an address without lifting a finger.'

The letter had indeed been written on stationery from the Addison Hotel, one of the city's lesser-known fleabags, some

two blocks north of the Eleventh Street Theatre, where
Mercy Howell had worked. There was a single sheet of paper
in the envelope. Carella unfolded it. Lettered in pencil were
the words:

PUT ON YOUR
CLOSE, MISS!
The Avenging Angel

The lamp went out, the room was black.

At first there was no sound but the sharp intake of Adele
Gorman's breath. And then, indistinctly, as faintly as
though carried on a swirling mist that blew in wetly from
some desolated shore, there came the sound of garbled
voices, and the room grew suddenly cold. The voices were
those of a crowd in endless debate, rising and falling in ca-
cophonous cadence, a mixture of tongues that rattled and
rasped. There was the sound, too, of a rising wind, as though
a door to some forbidden landscape had been sharply and
suddenly blown open (how cold the room was!) to reveal a
host of corpses incessantly pacing, involved in formless dia-
logue. The voices rose in volume now, carried on that same
chill penetrating wind, louder, closer, until they seemed to
overwhelm the room, clamouring to be released from whatever unearthly vault contained them. And then, as if two
and only two of those disembodied voices had succeeded in

breaking away from the mass of unseen dead, bringing with them a rush of bone-chilling air from some world unknown, there came a whisper at first, the whisper of a man's voice, saying the single word 'Ralph!' sharp-edged and with a distinctive foreign inflection, 'Ralph!' and then a woman's voice joining it, 'Adele!' pronounced strangely and in the same cutting whisper, 'Adele!' and then 'Ralph!' again, the voices overlapping, unmistakably foreign, urgent, rising in volume until the whispers commingled to become an agonizing groan and the names were lost in the shrilling echo of the wind.

Meyer's eyes played tricks in the darkness. Apparitions that surely were not there seemed to float on the crescendo of sound that saturated the room. Barely perceived pieces of furniture assumed amorphous shapes as the male voice snarled and the female voice moaned above it in contralto counterpoint. And then the babel of other voices intruded again, as though calling these two back to whatever grim mossy crypt they had momentarily escaped. The sound of the wind became more fierce, and the voices of those numberless pacing dead receded, and echoed, and were gone.

The lamp sputtered back into dim illumination. The room seemed perceptibly warmer, but Meyer Meyer was covered with a cold clammy sweat.

'*Now* do you believe?' Adele Gorman asked.

Detective Bob O'Brien was coming out of the men's room down the hall when he saw the woman sitting on the bench just outside the squad-room. He almost went back into the toilet, but he was an instant too late; she had seen him, there was no escape.

'Hello, Mr O'Brien,' she said, and performed an awkward little half-rising motion, as though uncertain whether she should stand to greet him or accept the deference due a lady. The clock on the squad-room wall read 3.02 AM, but the lady was dressed as though for a brisk afternoon's hike in the park, brown slacks and low-heeled walking shoes, brief beige car coat, a scarf around her head. She was perhaps fifty-five or thereabouts, with a face that once must have been pretty, save for the overlong nose. Green-eyed, with prominent cheekbones and a generous mouth, she executed her abortive rise, and then fell into step beside O'Brien as he walked into the squad-room.

'Little late in the night to be out, isn't it, Mrs Blair?' O'Brien asked. He was not an insensitive cop, but his manner now was brusque and dismissive. Faced with Mrs Blair for perhaps the seventeenth time in a month, he tried not to empathize with her loss because, truthfully, he was unable to assist her, and his inability to do so was frustrating.

'Have you seen her?' Mrs Blair asked.

'No,' O'Brien said. 'I'm sorry, Mrs Blair, but I haven't.'

'I have a new picture, perhaps that will help.'

'Yes, perhaps it will,' he said.

The telephone was ringing. He lifted the receiver and said, 'Eighty-seventh Squad, O'Brien here.'

'Bob, this's Bert Kling over on Culver, the church bombing.'

'Yeah, Bert.'

'Seems I remember seeing a red Volkswagen on that hot car bulletin we got yesterday. You want to dig it out and let me know where it was snatched?'

'Yeah, just a second,' O'Brien said, and began scanning the sheet on his desk.

'Here's the new picture,' Mrs Blair said. 'I know you're very good with runaways, Mr O'Brien, the kids all like you and give you information. If you see Penelope, all I want you to do is tell her I love her and am sorry for the misunderstanding.'

'Yeh, I will,' O'Brien said. Into the phone, he said, 'I've got two red VWs, Bert, a '64 and a '66. You want them both?'

'Shoot,' Kling said.

'The '64 was stolen from a guy named Art Hauser. It was parked outside 861 West Meridian.'

'And the '66?'

'Owner is a woman named Alice Cleary. Car was stolen from a parking lot on Fourteenth.'

'North or South?'

'South. 303 South.'

'Right. Thanks, Bob,' Kling said, and hung up.

'And ask her to come home to me,' Mrs Blair said.

'Yes, I will,' O'Brien said. 'If I see her. I certainly will.'

'That's a nice picture of Penny, don't you think?' Mrs Blair asked. 'It was taken last Easter. It's the most recent picture I have. I thought it would be most helpful to you.'

O'Brien looked at the girl in the picture, and then looked up into Mrs Blair's green eyes, misted now with tears, and suddenly wanted to reach across the desk and pat her hand reassuringly, the one thing he could *not* do with any honesty. Because whereas it was true that he was the squad's runaway expert, with perhaps fifty snapshots of teenage boys and girls crammed into his bulging notebook, and whereas his record of finds was more impressive than any other cop's in the city, uniformed or plain-clothes, there wasn't a damn thing he could do for the mother of Penelope Blair, who had run away from home last June.

'You understand . . .' he started to say.

'Let's not go into *that* again, Mr O'Brien,' she said, and rose.

'Mrs Blair . . .'

'I don't want to hear it,' Mrs Blair said, walking quickly out of the squad-room. 'Tell her to come home. Tell her I love her,' she said, and was gone down the iron-runged steps.

O'Brien sighed and stuffed the new picture of Penelope into his notebook. What Mrs Blair did not choose to hear again was the fact that her runaway daughter Penny was twenty-four years old, and there was not a single agency on God's green earth, police or otherwise, that could force her to go home again if she did not choose to.

Fats Donner was a stool pigeon with a penchant for Turkish

baths. A mountainous white Buddha of a man, he could usually be found at one or another of the city's steam emporiums at any given hour of the day, draped in a towel and revelling in the heat that saturated his flabby body. Bert Kling found him in an all-night place called Steam-Fit. He sent the masseur into the steam room to tell Donner he was there, and Donner sent word out that he would be through in five minutes, unless Kling wished to join him. Kling did not wish to join him. He waited in the locker room, and in seven minutes' time, Donner came out, draped in his customary towel, a ludicrous sight at *any* time, but particularly at close to 3.30 AM.

'Hey!' Donner said. 'How you doing?'

'Fine,' Kling said. 'How about yourself?'

'*Comme ci, comme ça,*' Donner said, and made a seesawing motion with one fleshy hand.

'I'm looking for some stolen heaps,' Kling said, getting directly to the point.

'What kind?' Donner said.

'Volkswagens. A '64 and a '66.'

'What colour are they?'

'Red.'

'Both of them?'

'Yes.'

'Where were they heisted?'

'One from in front of 861 West Meridian. The other from a parking lot on South Fourteenth.'

'When was this?'

'Both last week sometime. I don't have the exact dates.'

'What do you want to know?'

'Who stole them.'

'You think it's the same guy on both?'

'I doubt it.'

'What's so important about these heaps?'

'One of them may have been used in a bombing tonight.'

'You mean the church over on Culver?'

'That's right.'

'Count me out,' Donner said.

'What do you mean?'

'There's a lot of guys in this town who're in *sympathy* with what happened over there tonight. I don't want to get involved in none of this black-white shit.'

'Who's going to know whether you're involved or not?' Kling asked.

'The same way *you* get information, *they* get information.'

'I need your help, Donner.'

'Yeah, well, I'm sorry on this one,' Donner said, and shook his head.

'In that case, I'd better hurry down to High Street.'

'Why? You got another source down there?'

'No, that's where the DA's office is.'

Both men stared at each other, Donner in a white towel draped around his belly, sweat still pouring from his face and his chest even though he was no longer in the steam room, Kling looking like a slightly tired advertising executive rather than a cop threatening a man with revelation of past deeds not entirely legal. They stared at each other with total understanding, caught in the curious symbiosis of law breaker and law enforcer, an empathy created by neither man, but essential to the existence of both. It was Donner who broke the silence.

'I don't like being coerced,' he said.

'I don't like being refused,' Kling answered.

'When do you need this?'

'I want to get going on it before morning.'

'You expect miracles, don't you?'

'Doesn't everybody?'

'Miracles cost.'

'How much?'

'Twenty-five if I turn up one heap, fifty if I turn up both.'

'Turn them up first. We'll talk later.'

'And if somebody breaks my head later?'

'You should have thought of that before you entered the profession,' Kling said. 'Come on, Donner, cut it out. This is a routine bombing by a couple of punks. You've got nothing to be afraid of.'

'No?' Donner asked. And then, in a very professorial voice, he uttered perhaps the biggest understatement of the decade. 'Racial tensions are running very high in this city right now.'

'Have you got my number at the squad-room?'

'Yeah, I've got it,' Donner said glumly.

'I'm going back there now. Let me hear from you soon.'

'You mind if I get dressed first?' Donner asked.

The night clerk at the Addison Hotel was alone in the lobby when Carella and Hawes walked in. Immersed in an open book on the desk in front of him, he did not look up as they approached. The lobby was furnished in faded Gothic: a threadbare oriental rug, heavy curliced mahogany tables, ponderous stuffed chairs with sagging bottoms and soiled antimacassars, two spittoons resting alongside each of two mahogany-panelled supporting columns. A real Tiffany lampshade hung over the registration desk, one leaded glass panel gone, another badly cracked. In the old days, the Addison had been a luxury hotel. It now wore its past splendour with all the style of a two-dollar hooker in a moth-eaten mink she'd picked up in a thrift shop.

The clerk, in contrast to his ancient surroundings, was a young man in his mid-twenties, wearing a neatly pressed brown tweed suit, a tan shirt, a gold-and-brown silk rep tie, and eyeglasses with tortoiseshell rims. He glanced up at the detectives belatedly, squinting after the intense concentration of peering at print, and then he got to his feet.

'Yes, gentlemen,' he said. 'May I help you?'

'Police officers,' Carella said. He took his wallet from his pocket, and opened it to where his detective's shield was pinned to a leather flap.

'Yes, sir.'

'I'm Detective Carella, this is my partner Detective Hawes.'

'How do you do? I'm the night clerk, my name is Ronnie Sanford.'

'We're looking for someone who may have been registered here two weeks ago,' Hawes said.

'Well, if he was registered here two weeks ago,' Sanford said, 'chances are he's still registered. Most of our guests are residents.'

'Do you keep stationery in the lobby here?' Carella asked.

'Sir?'

'Stationery. Is there any place here in the lobby where someone could walk in off the street and pick up a piece of stationery?'

'No, sir. There's a writing desk there in the corner, near the staircase, but we don't stock it with stationery, no, sir.'

'Is there stationery in the rooms?'

'Yes, sir.'

'How about here at the desk?'

'Yes, of course, sir.'

'Is there someone at this desk twenty-four hours a day?'

'Twenty-four hours a day, yes, sir. We have three shifts. Eight to four in the afternoon. Four to midnight. And midnight to eight AM.'

'You came on at midnight, did you?'

'Yes, sir.'

'Any guests come in after you started your shift?'

'A few, yes, sir.'

'Notice anybody with blood on his clothes?'

'Blood? Oh, no, sir.'

'*Would* you have noticed?'

'What do you mean?'

'Are you generally pretty aware of what's going on around here?'

'I try to be, sir. At least, for most of the night. I catch a little nap when I'm not studying, but usually . . .'

'What do you study?'

'Accounting.'

'Where?'

'At Ramsey U.'

'Mind if we take a look at your register?'

'Not at all, sir.'

He walked to the mail rack and took the hotel register from the counter there. Returning to the desk, he opened it, and said, 'All of our present guests are residents, with the exception of Mr Lambert in 204, and Mrs Grant in 701.'

'When did they check in?'

'Mr Lambert checked in . . . last night, I think it was. And Mrs Grant has been here for four days. She's leaving on Tuesday.'

'Are these the actual signatures of your guests?'

'Yes, sir. All guests are asked to sign the register, as required by state law.'

'Have you got that note, Cotton?' Carella asked, and then turned again to Sanford. 'Would you mind if we took this over to the couch there?'

'Well, we're not supposed . . .'

'We can give you a receipt for it, if you like.'

'No, I guess it'll be all right.'

They carried the register to a couch upholstered in faded red velvet. With the book supported on Carella's lap, they unfolded the note Mercy Howell had received, and began comparing the signatures of the guests with the only part of the note that was not written in block letters, the words 'The Avenging Angel'.

There were fifty-two guests in the hotel. Carella and Hawes went through the register once, and then started through it a second time.

'Hey,' Hawes said suddenly.

'What?'

'Look at this one.'

He took the note and placed it on the page so that it was directly above one of the signatures:

PUT ON YOUR CLOSE, MISS!

The Avenging Angel

Timothy Allen Ames

'What do you think?' he asked.
'Different handwriting,' Carella said.
'Same initials,' Hawes said.

Detective Meyer Meyer was still shaken. He did not like ghosts. He did not like this house. He wanted to go home. He wanted to be in bed with his wife Sarah. He wanted her to stroke his hand and tell him that such things did not exist, there was nothing to be afraid of, a grown man! How could he believe in poltergeists, shades, Dutch spirits? Ridiculous.

But he had heard them, and he had felt their chilling presence, and had almost thought he'd seen them, if only for an instant. He turned with fresh shock now towards the hall staircase and the sound of descending footsteps. Eyes wide, he waited for whatever new manifestation might present itself. He was tempted to draw his revolver, but he was afraid such an act would appear foolish to the Gormans. He had come here a sceptic, and he was now at least *willing* to believe, and he waited in dread for whatever was coming down those steps with such ponderous footfalls – some ghoul trailing winding sheets and rattling chains? some spectre with a bleached skull for a head and long bony clutching fingers dripping the blood of babies?

Willem Van Houten, wearing his red velvet slippers and his red smoking jacket, his hair still jutting wildly from behind each ear, his blue eyes fierce and snapping, came into the living-room and walked directly to where his daughter and son-in-law were sitting.

'Well?' he asked. 'Did they come again?'

'Yes, Daddy,' Adele said.

'What did they want this time?'

'I don't know. They spoke Dutch again.'

'Bastards,' Van Houten said, and then turned to Meyer. 'Did you see them?' he asked.

'No, sir, I did not,' Meyer said.

'But they were *here*,' Gorman protested, and turned his blank face to his wife. 'I heard them.'

'Yes, darling,' Adele assured him. 'We *all* heard them. But it was like that other time, don't you remember? When we could hear them even though they couldn't quite break through.'

'Yes, that's right,' Gorman said, and nodded. 'This happened once before, Detective Meyer.' He was facing Meyer now, his head tilted quizzically, the sightless eyes covered with their black reflecting glasses. When he spoke, his voice was like that of a child seeking reassurance. 'But you *did* hear them, didn't you, Detective Meyer?'

'Yes,' Meyer said. 'I heard them, Mr Gorman.'

'And the wind?'

'Yes, the wind, too.'

'And felt them? It ... it gets so cold when they appear. You *did* feel their presence, didn't you?'

'I felt something,' Meyer said.

Van Houten suddenly asked, 'Are you satisfied?'

'About what?' Meyer said.

'That there are ghosts in this house? That's why you're here, isn't it? To ascertain . . .'

'He's here because I asked Adele to contact the police,' Gorman said.

'Why did you do that?'

'Because of the stolen jewellery,' Gorman said. 'And because . . .' He paused. 'Because I . . . I've lost my sight, yes, but I wanted to . . . to make sure I wasn't losing my mind as well.'

'You're quite sure, Ralph,' Van Houten said.

'About the jewellery . . .' Meyer said.

'*They* took it,' Van Houten said.

'Who?'

'Johann and Elisabeth. Our friendly neighbourhood ghosts, the bastards.'

'That's impossible, Mr Van Houten.'

'Why is it impossible?'

'Because ghosts . . .' Meyer started, and hesitated.

'Yes?'

'Ghosts, well, ghosts don't go around stealing jewellery. I mean, what use would they have for it?' he said lamely, and looked at the Gormans for corroboration. Neither of them seemed to be in a supportive mood. They sat on the sofa near the fireplace, looking glum and defeated.

'They want us out of this house,' Van Houten said. 'It's as simple as that.'

'How do you know?'

'Because they said so.'

'When?'

'Before they stole the necklace and the earrings.'

'They told this to you?'

'To me and to my children. All three of us were here.'

'But I understand the ghosts speak only Dutch.'

'Yes, I translated for Ralph and Adele.'

'And then what happened?'

'What do you mean?'

'When did you discover the jewellery was missing?'

'The very instant they were gone.'

'You mean you went to the safe . . .'

'Yes, and opened it, and the jewellery was gone.'

'We had put it in the safe not ten minutes before that,' Adele said. 'We'd been to a party, Ralph and I, and we got home very late, and Daddy was still awake, reading, sitting in that chair you're in this very minute. I asked him to open the safe, and he did, and he put the jewellery in, and closed the safe and . . . and then *they* came and . . . and made their threats.'

'What time was this?'

'The usual time. The time they always come. Two forty-five in the morning.'

'And you say the jewellery was put into the safe at what time?'

'About two-thirty,' Gorman said.

'And when was the safe opened again?'

'Immediately after they left. They only stay a few moments. This time they told my father-in-law they were taking the necklace and the earrings with them. He rushed to the safe as soon as the lights came on again . . .'

'Do the lights always go off?'

'Always,' Adele said. 'It's always the same. The lights go off, and the room gets very cold, and we hear these . . . strange voices arguing.' She paused. 'And then Johann and Elisabeth come.'

'Except that *this* time they didn't come,' Meyer said.

'And one other time,' Adele said quickly.

'They want us out of this house,' Van Houten said, 'that's all there is to it. Maybe we *ought* to leave. Before they take *everything* from us.'

'Everything? What do you mean?'

'The rest of my daughter's jewellery. Some stock certificates. Everything that's in the safe.'

'Where *is* the safe?' Meyer asked.

'Here. Behind this painting.' Van Houten walked to the wall opposite the fireplace. An oil painting of a pastoral landscape hung there in an ornate gilt frame. The frame was hinged to the wall. Van Houten swung the painting out as though opening a door, and revealed the small, round, black safe behind it. 'Here,' he said.

'How many people know the combination?' Meyer asked.

'Just me,' Van Houten said.

'Do you keep the number written down anywhere?'

'Yes.'

'Where?'

'Hidden.'

'Where?'

'I hardly think that's any of your business, Detective Meyer.'

'I'm only trying to find out whether some other person could have got hold of the combination somehow.'

'Yes, I suppose that's possible,' Van Houten said. 'But highly unlikely.'

'Well,' Meyer said, and shrugged. 'I don't really know what to say. I'd like to measure the room, if you don't mind, get the dimensions, placement of doors and windows, things like that. For my report.' He shrugged again.

'It's rather late, isn't it?' Van Houten said.

'Well, I *got* here rather late,' Meyer said, and smiled.

'Come, Daddy, I'll make us all some tea in the kitchen,' Adele said. 'Will you be long, Detective Meyer?'

'I don't know. It may take a while.'

'Shall I bring you some tea?'

'Thank you, that would be nice.'

She rose from the couch and then guided her husband's hand to her arm. Walking slowly beside him, she led him past her father and out of the room. Van Houten looked at Meyer once again, nodded briefly, and followed them out. Meyer closed the door behind them and immediately walked to the standing floor lamp.

The woman was sixty years old, and she looked like any-body's grandmother, except that she had just murdered her husband and three children. They had explained her rights to her, and she had told them she had nothing to hide and would answer any questions they chose to ask. She sat in a straight-backed squad-room chair, wearing a black cloth coat over bloodstained pyjamas and robe, her handcuffed hands in her lap, her hands unmoving on her black leather pocketbook. O'Brien and Kling looked at the police stenographer, who glanced up at the wall clock, noted the time of the interrogation's start as 3.55 AM, and then signalled that he was ready whenever they were.

'What is your name?' O'Brien asked.

'Isabel Martin.'

'How old are you, Mrs Martin?'

'Sixty.'

'Where do you live?'

'On Ainsley Avenue.'

'Where on Ainsley?'

'657 Ainsley.'

'With whom do you live there?'

'With my husband Roger, and my son Peter, and my daughters Annie and Abigail.'

'Would you like to tell us what happened tonight, Mrs Martin?' Kling asked.

'I killed them all,' she said. She had white hair, a fine aquiline nose, brown eyes behind rimless spectacles. She stared straight ahead of her as she spoke, looking neither to her right nor to her left, ignoring her questioners completely, seemingly alone with the memory of what she had done not a half-hour before.

'Can you give us some of the details, Mrs Martin?'

'I killed *him* first, the son of a bitch.'

'Who do you mean, Mrs Martin?'

'My husband.'

'When was this?'

'When he came home.'

'What time was that, do you remember?'

'A little while ago.'

'It's almost four o'clock now,' Kling said. 'Would you say this was at, what, three-thirty or thereabouts?'

'I didn't look at the clock,' she said. 'I heard his key in the latch, and I went in the kitchen, and there he was.'

'Yes?'

'There's a meat cleaver I keep on the sink. I hit him with it.'

'Why did you do that, Mrs Martin?'

'Because I wanted to.'

'Were you arguing with him, is that it?'

'No. He was locking the door, and I just went over to the sink and picked up the cleaver, and then I hit him with it.'

'Where did you hit him, Mrs Martin?'

'On his head and on his neck and I think on his shoulder.'

'You hit him three times with the cleaver?'

'I hit him a lot of times, I don't know how many times.'

'Were you aware that you were hitting him?'

'Yes, I was aware.'

'You knew you were striking him with a cleaver?'

'Yes, I knew.'

'Did you intend to kill him with the cleaver?'

'I intended to kill him with the cleaver.'

'And afterwards, did you know you had killed him?'

'I knew he was dead, yes, the son of a bitch.'

'What did you do then?'

'My oldest child came into the kitchen. Peter. My son. He yelled at me, he wanted to know what I'd done, he kept yelling at me. I hit him, too, to get him to shut up. I hit him only once, across the throat.'

'Did you know what you were doing at the time?'

'I knew what I was doing. He was *another* one, that Peter. Little bastard.'

'What happened next, Mrs Martin?'

'I went in the back bedroom where the two girls sleep, and I hit Annie with the cleaver first, and then I hit Abigail.'

'Where did you hit them, Mrs Martin?'

'On the face. Their faces.'

'How many times?'

'I think I hit Annie twice, and Abigail only once.'

'Why did you do that, Mrs Martin?'

'Who would take care of them after I was gone?' Mrs Martin asked of no one.

'Is there anything else you want to tell us?' Kling asked.

'There's nothing more to tell. I done the right thing.'

The detectives walked away from the desk. They were both pale. 'Man,' O'Brien whispered.

'Yeah,' Kling said. 'We'd better call the night DA right away, get him to take a full confession from her.'

'Killed four of them without batting an eyelash,' O'Brien said, and shook his head, and went back to where the stenographer was typing up Mrs Martin's statement.

The telephone was ringing. Kling walked to the nearest desk and lifted the receiver. 'Eighty-seventh Squad, Detective Kling,' he said.

'This is Donner.'

'Yeah, Fats.'

'I think I got a lead on one of those heaps.'

'Shoot.'

'This would be the one heisted on Fourteenth Street. According to the dope I've got, it happened yesterday morning. Does that check out?'

'I'll have to look at the bulletin again. Go ahead, Fats.'

'It's already been ditched,' Donner said. 'If you're looking for it, try outside the electric company on the River Road.'

'Thanks, I'll make a note of that. Who stole it, Fats?'

'This is strictly *entre nous*,' Donner said. 'I don't want *no* tie-in with it *never*. The guy who done it is a mean little bastard, rip out his mother's heart for a dime. He hates niggers, killed two of them in a street rumble four years ago, and managed to beat the rap. I think maybe some officer was on the take, huh, Kling?'

'You can't square homicide in this city, and you know it, Fats.'

'Yeah? I'm surprised. You can square damn near anything else for a couple of bills.'

'What's his name?'

'Danny Ryder. 3541 Grover Avenue, near the park. You won't find him there now, though.'

'Where *will* I find him now?'

'Ten minutes ago, he was in an all-night bar on Mason, place called Felicia's. You going in after him?'

'I am.'

'Take your gun,' Donner said.

There were seven people in Felicia's when Kling got there at a quarter to five. He cased the bar through the plate-glass window fronting the place, unbuttoned the third button of his overcoat, reached in to clutch the butt of his revolver, worked it out of the holster once and then back again, and went in through the front door.

There was the immediate smell of stale cigarette smoke and beer and sweat and cheap perfume. A Puerto Rican girl was in whispered consultation with a sailor in one of the leatherette booths. Another sailor was hunched over the jukebox, thoughtfully considering his next selection, his face tinted orange and red and green from the coloured tubing. A tired, fat, fifty-year old blonde sat at the far end of the bar, watching the sailor as though the next button he pushed might destroy the entire world. The bartender was polishing glasses. He looked up when Kling walked in and immediately smelled the law.

Two men were seated at the opposite end of the bar.

One of them was wearing a blue turtleneck sweater, grey slacks, and desert boots. His brown hair was cut close to his scalp in a military cut. The other man was wearing a bright orange team jacket, almost luminous, with the words *Orioles, SAC* lettered across its back in Old English script. The one with the crew cut said something softly, and the other one chuckled. Behind the bar, a glass clinked as the bartender replaced it on the shelf. The jukebox erupted in sound, Jimi Hendrix rendering *All Along the Watchtower*.

Kling walked over to the two men.

'Which one of you is Danny Ryder?' he asked.

The one with the short hair said, 'Who wants to know?'

'Police officer,' Kling said, and the one in the orange jacket whirled with a pistol in his hand, and Kling's eyes opened wide in surprise, and the gun went off.

There was no time to think, there was hardly any time to breathe. The explosion of the gun was shockingly close, the acrid stink of cordite rushed into his nostrils. The knowledge that he was still alive, the sweet rushing clean awareness that the bullet had somehow missed him was only a fleeting click of intelligence accompanying what was essentially a reflexive act. The .38 came free of its holster, his finger was inside the trigger guard and around the trigger, he squeezed off his shot almost before the gun had cleared the flap of his overcoat, fired into the orange jacket and threw his shoulder simultaneously against the chest of the man with the short hair, knocking him backwards off his stool. The man in the orange jacket, his face twisted in pain, was levelling the gun for another shot. Kling fired again, squeezing the trigger without thought or rancour, and then whirling on the man with the short hair, who was crouched on the floor against the bar.

'Get up!' he yelled.

'Don't shoot.'

'Get up, you son of a bitch!'

He yanked the man to his feet, hurled him against the bar, thrust the muzzle of his pistol at the blue turtleneck sweater, ran his hands under the armpits and between the legs while the man kept saying over and over again, 'Don't shoot, please don't shoot.'

He backed away from him and leaned over the one in the orange jacket.

'Is this Ryder?' he asked.

'Yes.'

'Who're you?'

'Frank . . . Frank Pasquale. Look, I . . .'

'Shut up, Frank,' Kling said. 'Put your hands behind your back! Move!'

He had already taken his handcuffs from his belt. He snapped them on to Pasquale's wrists now, and only then became aware that Jimi Hendrix was still singing, the sailors were watching with pale white faces, the Puerto Rican girl was screaming, the fat faded blonde had her mouth open, the bartender was frozen in mid-motion, the tip of his bar towel inside a glass.

'All right,' Kling said. He was breathing harshly. 'All right,' he said again, and wiped his forehead.

Timothy Allen Ames was a pot-bellied man of forty, with a thick black moustache, a mane of long black hair, and brown eyes sharply alert at five minutes past five in the morning. He answered the door as though he'd been already awake, asked for identification, and then asked the detectives to wait a moment, and closed the door, and came back shortly afterwards, wearing a robe over his striped pyjamas.

'Is your name Timothy Ames?' Carella asked.

'That's me,' Ames said. 'Little late to be paying a visit, ain't it?'

'Or early, depending how you look at it,' Hawes said.

'One thing I can do without at five AM is humorous cops,' Ames said. 'How'd you get up here, anyway? Is that little jerk asleep at the desk again?'

'Who do you mean?' Carella asked.

'Lonnie Sanford, whatever the hell his name is.'

'*Ronnie* Sanford.'

'Yeah, him. Little bastard's always giving me trouble.'

'What kind of trouble?'

'About broads,' Ames said. 'Acts like he's running a nunnery here, can't stand to see a guy come in with a girl. I notice he ain't got no compunctions about letting *cops* upstairs, though, no matter *what* time it is.'

'Never mind Sanford, let's talk about you,' Carella said.

'Sure, what would you like to know?'

'Where were you between eleven-twenty and twelve o'clock tonight?'

'Right here.'

'Can you prove it?'

'Sure. I got back here about eleven o'clock, and I been here since. Ask Sanford downstairs ... no, never mind, he wasn't on yet. He don't come on till midnight.'

'Who *else* can we ask, Ames?'

'Listen, you going to make trouble for me?'

'Only if you're *in* trouble.'

'I got a broad here. She's over eighteen, don't worry. But, like, she's a junkie, you know? She ain't holding or nothing, but I know you guys, and if you want to make trouble ...'

'Where is she?'

'In the john.'

'Get her out here.'

'Look, do me a favour, will you? Don't bust the kid. She's trying to kick the habit, she really is. I been helping her along.'

'How?'

'By keeping her busy,' Ames said, and winked.

'Call her.'

'Bea, come out here!' Ames shouted.

There was a moment's hesitation, and then the bathroom door opened. The girl was a tall, plain brunette wearing a short terry cloth robe. She sidled into the room cautiously, as though expecting to be struck in the face at any moment. Her brown eyes were wide with expectancy. She knew fuzz, and she knew what it was like to be busted on a narcotics charge, and she had listened to the conversation from behind the closed bathroom door, and now she waited for whatever was coming, expecting the worst.

'What's your name, miss?' Hawes asked.

'Beatrice Norden.'

'What time did you get here tonight, Beatrice?'

'About eleven.'

'Was this man with you?'

'Yes.'

'Did he leave here at any time tonight?'

'No.'

'Are you sure?'

'I'm positive. He picked me up about nine o'clock ...'

'Where do you live, Beatrice?'

'Well, that's the thing, you see,' the girl said. 'I been put out of my room.'

'So where'd he pick you up?'

'At my girlfriend's house. You can ask her, she was there when he came. Her name is Rosalie Dewes. Anyway, Timmy picked me up at nine, and we went to eat at Chink's, and we came up here around eleven.'

'I hope you're telling us the truth, Miss Norden,' Carella said.

'I swear to God, we been here all night,' Beatrice answered.

'All right, Ames,' Hawes said, 'we'd like a sample of your handwriting.'

'My *what*?'

'Your handwriting.'

'What for?'

'We collect autographs,' Carella said.

'Gee, these guys really break me up,' Ames said to the girl. 'Regular nightclub comics we get in the middle of the night.'

Carella handed him a pen and then tore a sheet from his pad. 'You want to write this for me?' he said. 'The first part's in block lettering.'

'What the hell is block lettering?' Ames asked.

'He means *print* it,' Hawes said.

'Then why didn't he say so?'

'Put on your clothes, miss,' Carella said.

'What for?' Beatrice said. 'I mean, the thing is, I was in bed when you guys . . .'

'That's what I want him to write,' Carella explained.

'Oh.'

'Put on your clothes, miss,' Ames repeated, and lettered it on to the sheet of paper. 'What else?' he asked, looking up.

'Now sign it in your own handwriting with the following words: The Avenging Angel.'

'What the hell is this supposed to be?' Ames asked.

'You want to write it, please?'

Ames wrote the words, and then handed the slip of paper to Carella. He and Hawes compared it with the note that had been mailed to Mercy Howell:

PUT ON YOUR CLOSE, MISS!

The Avenging Angel

PUT ON YOUR CLOTHES, MISS.

The Avenging Angel

'So?' Ames asked.

'So you're clean,' Hawes said.

'Imagine if I was dirty,' Ames answered.

At the desk downstairs, Ronnie Sanford was still immersed in his accounting textbook. He got to his feet again as the detectives came out of the elevator, adjusted his glasses on his nose, and then said, 'Any luck?'

'Afraid not,' Carella answered. 'We're going to need this register for a while, if that's okay.'

'Well...'

'Give him a receipt for it, Cotton,' Carella said. It was late, and he didn't want a debate in the lobby of a run-down hotel. Hawes quickly made out a receipt in duplicate, signed both copies and handed one to Sanford.

'What about this torn cover?' Hawes asked belatedly.

'Yeah,' Carella said. There was a small rip on the leather binding of the book, and he fingered it briefly now, and then said, 'Better note that on the receipt, Cotton.' Hawes took back the receipt and, on both copies, jotted the words 'Small rip on front cover'. He handed the receipts back to Sanford.

'Want to just sign these, Mr Sanford?' he said.

'What for?' Sanford asked.

'To indicate we received the register in this condition.'

'Oh, sure,' Sanford said. He picked up a ball-point pen from its desk holder, and asked, 'What do you want me to write?'

'Your name and your title, that's all.'

'My title?'

'Night Clerk, the Addison Hotel.'

'Oh, sure,' Sanford said, and signed both receipts. 'This okay?' he asked. The detectives looked at what he had written.

'You like girls?' Carella asked suddenly.

'What?' Sanford asked.

'Girls,' Hawes said.

'Sure. Sure, I like girls.'

'Dressed or naked?'

'What?'

'With clothes or without?'

'I . . . I don't know what you mean, sir.'

'Where were you tonight between eleven-twenty and mid-night?' Hawes asked.

'Getting . . . getting ready to come to . . . to work,' Sanford said.

'You sure you weren't in the alley of the Eleventh Street Theatre stabbing a girl named Mercy Howell?'

'What? No . . . no, of course . . . of course not. I was . . . I was . . . I was home . . . getting . . . getting dressed . . . to . . . to . . .' Sanford took a deep breath and decided to get indignant. 'Listen, what's this all about?' he said. 'Would you mind telling me?'

'It's all about *this*,' Carella said, and turned one of the receipts so that Sanford could read the signature:

Ronald Sanford
Night Clerk
The Addison Hotel

'Get your hat,' Hawes said. 'Study hall's over.'

It was twenty-five minutes past five when Adele Gorman came into the room with Meyer's cup of tea. He was crouched near the air-conditioning unit recessed into the wall to the left of the curtains, and he glanced over his shoulder when he heard her, and then rose.

'I didn't know what you took,' she said, 'so I brought every-thing.'

'Thank you,' he said. 'Just a little milk and sugar is fine.'

'Have you measured the room?' she asked, and put the tray down on the table in front of the sofa.

'Yes, I think I have everything I need now,' Meyer said. He put a spoonful of sugar into the tea, stirred it, added a drop of milk, stirred it again, and then lifted the cup to his mouth. 'Hot,' he said.

Adele Gorman was watching him silently. She said nothing. He kept sipping his tea. The ornate clock on the mantelpiece ticked in a swift whispering tempo.

'Do you always keep this room so dim?' Meyer asked.

'Well, my husband is blind, you know,' Adele said. 'There's really no need for brighter light.'

'Mmm. But your father reads in this room, doesn't he?'

'I beg your pardon?'

'The night you came home from that party. He was sitting in the chair over there near the floor lamp. Reading. Remember?'

'Oh. Yes, he was.'

'Bad light to read by.'

'Yes, I suppose it is.'

'I think maybe those bulbs are defective,' Meyer said.

'Do you think so?'

'Mmm. I happened to look at the lamp, and there are three hundred-watt bulbs in it, all of them burning. You should be getting a lot more illumination with that kind of wattage.'

'Well, I really don't know too much about . . .'

'Unless the lamp is on a rheostat, of course.'

'I'm afraid I don't know what a rheostat is.'

'It's an adjustable resistor. You can dim your lights or make them brighter with it. I thought maybe the lamp was on a rheostat, but I couldn't find a control knob anywhere in the room.' Meyer paused. 'You wouldn't know if there's a rheostat control someplace in the house, would you?'

'I'm sure there isn't,' Adele said.

'Must be defective bulbs then,' Meyer said, and smiled. 'Also, I think your air conditioner is broken.'

'No, I'm sure it isn't.'

'Well, I was just looking at it, and all the switches are turned to the "On" position, but it isn't working. So I guess it's broken. That's a shame, too, because it's such a nice unit. Sixteen thousand BTUs. That's a lot of cooling power for a room this size. We've got one of those big old price-fixed apartments on Concord, my wife and I, with a large bed-room, and we get adequate cooling from a half-ton unit. It's a shame this one is broken.'

'Yes. Detective Meyer, I don't wish to appear rude, but it *is* late . . .'

'Sure,' Meyer said. 'Unless, of course, the air conditioner's on a remote switch, too. So that all you have to do is turn a knob in another part of the house and it comes on.' He paused. '*Is* there such a switch someplace, Mrs Gorman?'

'I have no idea.'

'I'll just finish my tea and run along,' Meyer said. He lifted the cup to his lips, sipped at the tea, glanced at her over the rim, took the cup away from his mouth, and said, 'But I'll be back.'

'I hardly think there's any need for that,' Adele said.

'Well, some jewellery's been stolen . . .'

'The ghosts . . .'

'Come off it, Mrs Gorman.'

The room went silent.

'Where are the loudspeakers, Mrs Gorman?' Meyer asked. 'In the false beams up there? They're hollow, I checked them out.'

'I think perhaps you'd better leave,' Adele said slowly.

'Sure,' Meyer said. He put the teacup down, sighed, and got to his feet.

'I'll show you out,' Adele said.

They walked to the front door and out into the driveway. The night was still. The drizzle had stopped, and a thin layer of frost covered the grass rolling away towards the river below. Their footsteps crunched on the gravel as they walked slowly towards the automobile.

'My husband was blinded four years ago,' Adele said abruptly. 'He's a chemical engineer, there was an explosion at the plant, he could have been killed. Instead, he was only blinded.' She hesitated an instant, and then said again, 'Only blinded,' and there was such a sudden cry of despair in those two words that Meyer wanted to put his arm around her, console her the way he might his daughter, tell her that everything would be all right come morning, the night was almost done, and morning was on the horizon. He leaned on the fender of his car, and she stood beside him looking down at the driveway gravel, her eyes not meeting his. They could have been conspirators exchanging secrets in the night, but they were only two people who had been thrown together on a premise as flimsy as the ghosts that inhabited this house.

'He gets a disability pension from the company,' Adele said, 'they've really been quite kind to us. And, of course, I work. I teach school, Detective Meyer. Kindergarten. I love children.' She paused. She would not raise her eyes to meet his. 'But ... it's sometimes very difficult. My father, you see ...'

Meyer waited. He longed suddenly for dawn, but he waited patiently, and heard her catch her breath as though committed to go ahead now, however painful the revelation might be, compelled to throw herself upon the mercy of the night before the morning sun broke through.

'My father's been retired for fifteen years.' She took a deep breath, and then said, 'He gambles, Detective Meyer. He's a horse player. He loses large sums of money.'

'Is that why he stole your jewels?' Meyer asked.

'You know, don't you?' Adele said simply, and raised her eyes to his. 'Of course you know. It's quite transparent, his ruse, a shoddy little show really, a performance that would fool no one but ... no one but a blind man.' She brushed at her cheek; he could not tell whether the cold air had caused her sudden tears. 'I ... I really don't care about the theft, the jewels were left to me by my mother, and after all it was my father who bought them for her, so it's ... it's really like returning a legacy, I really don't care about that part of it. I ... I'd have *given* the jewellery to him if only he'd asked, but he's so proud, such a proud man. A proud man who ... who steals from me and pretends that ghosts are committing the crime. And my husband, in his dark universe, listens to the sounds my father puts on tape and visualizes things he cannot quite believe and so he asks me to contact the police because he needs an impartial observer to contradict the suspicion that someone is stealing pennies from his blind man's cup. That's why I came to you, Detective Meyer. So that you would arrive here tonight and perhaps be fooled as I was fooled at first, and perhaps say to my husband, "Yes, Mr Gorman, there *are* ghosts in your house." ' She suddenly placed her hand on his sleeve. The tears were streaming down her face, she had difficulty catching her breath. 'Because you see, Detective Meyer, there are ghosts in this house, there really and truly are. The ghost of a proud man who was once a brilliant judge and lawyer and who is now a gambler and a thief; and the ghost of a man who once could see, and who now trips and falls in ... in the darkness.'

On the river, a tugboat hooted. Adele Gorman fell silent. Meyer opened the door of his car and got in behind the wheel.

'I'll call your husband tomorrow,' he said abruptly and gruffly. 'Tell him I'm convinced something supernatural is happening here.'

'And will you be back, Detective Meyer?'

'No,' he said. 'I won't be back, Mrs Gorman.'

In the squad-room, they were wrapping up the night. Their day had begun at 7.45 PM yesterday, and they had been officially relieved at 5.45 AM, but they had not left the office yet because there were still questions to be asked, reports to be typed, odds and ends to put in place before they could go home. And since the relieving detectives were busy getting their approaching workday organized, the squad-room at 6 AM was busier than it might have been on any given afternoon, with two teams of cops getting in each other's way.

In the Interrogation Room, Carella and Hawes were questioning young Ronald Sanford in the presence of the assistant district attorney who had come over earlier to take Mrs Martin's confession, and who now found himself listening to another one when all he wanted to do was go home to sleep. Sanford seemed terribly shocked that they had been able to notice the identical handwriting in 'The Addison Hotel' and 'The Avenging Angel', he couldn't get over it. He thought he had been very clever in misspelling the word 'clothes', because then if they ever *had* traced the note, they would think some illiterate had written it, and not someone who was studying to be an accountant. He could not explain why he had killed Mercy Howell. He got all mixed up when he tried to explain that. It had something to do with the moral climate of America, and people exposing themselves in public, people like that shouldn't be allowed to pollute others, to foist their filth upon others, to intrude upon the privacy of others who only wanted to make a place for themselves in the world, who were trying so very hard to make something of themselves, studying accounting by day and working in a hotel by night, what right had these other people to ruin it for everybody else?

Frank Pasquale's tune, sung in the Clerical Office to Kling and O'Brien, was not quite so hysterical, but similar to Sanford's none the less. He had got the idea together with Danny Ryder. They had decided between them that the niggers in America were getting too damn pushy, shoving their way in where they didn't belong, taking jobs away from decent hard-working people who only wanted to be left alone, what right did they have to force themselves on everybody else? So they had decided to bomb the church, just to show the goddamn boogies that you couldn't get away with shit like that, not in America. He didn't seem too terribly concerned over the fact that his partner was lying stone cold dead on a slab at the morgue, or that their little Culver Avenue expedition had cost three people their lives, and had severely injured a half-dozen others. All he wanted to know, repeatedly, was whether his picture would be in the newspaper.

At his desk, Meyer Meyer started to type up a report on

the Gorman ghosts, and then decided the hell with it. If the lieutenant asked him where he'd been half the night, he would say he had been out cruising, looking for trouble in the streets. Christ knew there was enough of *that* around. He pulled the report forms and their separating sheets of carbon paper from the ancient typewriter, and noticed that Detective Hal Willis was pacing the room anxiously, waiting to get at the desk the moment he vacated it.

'Okay, Hal,' he said, 'it's all yours.'

'*Finalmente!*' Willis, who was not Italian, said.

The telephone rang.

The sun was up when they came out of the building and walked past the hanging green '87' globes and down the low flat steps to the sidewalk. The park across the street shimmered with early morning autumn brilliance, the sky above it clear and blue. It was going to be a beautiful day. They walked towards the diner on the next block, Meyer and O'Brien ahead of the others, Carella, Hawes, and Kling bringing up the rear. They were tired, and exhaustion showed in their eyes and in the set of their mouths, and in the pace they kept. They talked without animation, mostly about their work, their breaths feathery and white on the cold morning air. When they reached the diner, they took off their overcoats and ordered hot coffee and cheese, Danish, and toasted English muffins. Meyer said he thought he was coming down with a cold. Carella told him about some cough medicine his wife had given one of the children. O'Brien, munching on a muffin, glanced across the diner and saw a young girl in one of the booths. She was wearing blue jeans and a brightly coloured Mexican serape, and she was talking to a boy wearing a Navy pea jacket.

'I think I see somebody,' he said, and he moved out of the booth past Kling and Hawes, who were talking about the new goddamn regulation on search and seizure.

The girl looked up when he approached the booth.

'Miss Blair?' he said. 'Penelope Blair?'

'Yes,' the girl answered. 'Who are you?'

'Detective O'Brien,' he said, 'the Eighty-seventh Squad. Your mother was in last night, Penny. She asked me to tell you . . .'

'Flake off, cop,' Penelope Blair said. 'Go stop a riot someplace.'

O'Brien looked at her silently for a moment. He nodded then, and turned away, and went back to the table.

'Anything?' Kling asked.

'You can't win 'em all,' O'Brien said.

TWO

DAYWATCH

The boy who lay naked on the concrete in the backyard of the tenement was perhaps eighteen years old. He wore his hair quite long, and he had recently begun growing a beard. His hair and his beard were black. His body was very white, and the blood that oozed on to the concrete pavement beneath him was very red.

The superintendent of the building discovered him at two minutes before 6 AM, when he went to put his garbage in one of the cans out back. The boy was lying face down in his own blood, and the super did not recognize him. He was shocked, of course. He did not ordinarily discover naked dead men in the backyard when he went to put out his garbage. But considering his shock, and considering his advanced age (he was approaching eighty), he managed to notify the police with considerable dispatch, something not every good citizen of the city managed to do quite so well or so speedily.

Hal Willis arrived on the scene at fifteen minutes past six, accompanied by Richard Genero, who was the newest man on the squad, having been recently promoted from patrolman to Detective/3rd Grade. Forbes and Phelps, the two men from Homicide, were already there. It was Willis' contention that any pair of Homicide cops was the same as any other pair of Homicide cops. He had never, for example, seen Forbes and Phelps in the same room with Monoghan and Monroe. Was this not undeniable proof that they were one and the same couple? Moreover, it seemed to Willis that all Homicide cops exchanged clothing regularly, and that Forbes and Phelps could on any given day of the week be found wearing suits and overcoats belonging to Monoghan and Monroe.

'Good morning,' Willis said.

'Morning,' Phelps said.

Forbes grunted.

'Nice way to start a goddamn Sunday, right?' Phelps asked.

'You fellows got here pretty fast,' Genero said.

Forbes looked at him. 'Who're you?'

'Dick Genero.'

'Never heard of you,' Forbes said.

'I never heard of you, neither,' Genero answered, and glanced to Willis for approval.

'Who's the dead man?' Willis asked dryly. 'Anybody ever heard of *him*?'

'He sure as hell ain't carrying any identification,' Phelps said, and cackled hoarsely.

'Not unless he's got it shoved up his ass someplace,' Forbes said, and began laughing along with his partner.

'Who found the body?' Willis asked.

'Building superintendent.'

'Want to get him, Dick?'

'Right,' Genero said, and walked off.

'I hate to start my day like this,' Phelps said.

'Grisly,' Forbes said.

'All I had this morning was a cup of coffee,' Phelps said. 'And now *this*. Disgusting.'

'Nauseating,' Forbes said.

'Least have the decency to put on some goddamn clothes before he jumps off the roof,' Phelps said.

'How do you know he jumped off the roof?' Willis asked.

'I don't. I'm only saying.'

S–D

'What do you *think* he was doing?' Forbes asked. 'Walking around the backyard naked?'

'I don't know,' Willis said, and shrugged.

'Looks like a jumper to me,' Phelps said. He glanced up at the rear wall of the building. 'Isn't that a broken window up there?'

'Where?'

'Fourth floor there. Isn't that window broken there?'

'Looks like it,' Forbes said.

'Sure looks like it to me,' Phelps said.

'Hal, here's the super,' Genero said, approaching with the old man. 'Name's Mr Dennison, been working here for close to thirty years.'

'How do you do, Mr Dennison? I'm Detective Willis.'

Dennison nodded and said nothing.

'I understand you found the body.'

'That's right.'

'When was that?'

'Just before I called the cops.'

'What time was that, Mr Dennison?'

'Little after six, I guess.'

'Know who it is?'

'Can't see his face,' Dennison said.

'We'll roll him over for you as soon as the ME gets here,' Genero said.

'Don't do me no favours,' Dennison answered.

Unlike patrolmen, detectives – with the final approval of the Chief downtown – decide upon their own work schedules. As a result, the shifts will vary according to the whims of the men on the squad. For the past three months, and based on the dubious assumption that the night shift was more arduous than the day, the detectives of the 87th Squad had broken their working hours into two shifts, the first beginning at six in the morning and ending at eight in the evening, the second beginning then and ending at six the next day. The daywatch was fourteen hours long, the nightwatch only ten. But there were more men on duty during the day, and presumably this equalized the load. That some of those men were testifying in court or out on special assignments some of the time seemed not to bother any of the detectives, who considered the schedule equitable. At least for the time being. In another month or so, someone would come up with suggestions for a revised schedule, and they'd hold a meeting in the Interrogation Office and agree that they ought to try something new. A change was as good as a rest, provided the Chief approved.

As with any schedule, though, there were ways of beating it if you tried hard enough. Relieving the departing team at fifteen minutes before the hour was a mandatory courtesy, and one way of avoiding a 5.45 AM arrival at the squad-room was to plant yourself in a grocery store that did not open its doors until six-thirty. Detective Andy Parker found himself just such a grocery store on this bright October morning. The fact that the store had been robbed three times in broad daylight during the past month was only incidental. The point was that *some* detective had to cover the joint, and Andy Parker fortuitously happened to *be* that detective. The first thing he did to ingratiate himself with the owner was to swipe an apple from the fruit stand outside the store. The owner, one Silvio Corradini, who was sharp of eye for all his seventy-two years, noticed the petty larceny the moment it was committed. He was about to run out on the sidewalk to apprehend the brigand, when the man began walking directly into the store, eating the apple as he came. It was then that Silvio realized the man could be nothing but a cop.

'Good morning,' Parker said.

'Good morning,' Silvio replied. 'You enjoy the fruit?'

'Yeah, very good apple,' Parker said. 'Thanks a lot.' He grinned amiably. 'I'm Detective Parker,' he said, 'I've been assigned to these holdups.'

'What happened to the other detective?'

'Di Maeo? He's on vacation.'

'In October?'

'We can't all get the summertime, huh?' Parker said, and grinned again. He was a huge man wearing rumpled brown corduroy trousers and a soiled tan windbreaker. He had shaved this morning before eating breakfast, but he managed to look unshaven none the less. He bit into the apple ferociously, juice spilling onto his chin. Silvio, watching him, thought he resembled a hired gun for the Mafia.

'*Lei è italiano?*' he asked.

'What?'

'Are you Italian?'

'No, are you?' Parker said, and grinned.

'Yes,' Silvio answered. He drew back his shoulders. 'Yes, I'm Italian.'

'Well, good, good,' Parker said. 'You always open the store on Sunday?'

'What?'

'I said . . .'

'I only stay open till twelve o'clock, that's all,' Silvio said, and shrugged. 'I get the people coming home from church.'

'That's against the law in this state, you know that?'

'Nobody ever said anything.'

'Well, just because somebody's willing to look the other way every now and then, that doesn't make it legal,' Parker said. He stared deep into Silvio's eyes. 'We'll talk about it later, huh? Meantime, fill me in on these holdups, okay?'

Silvio hesitated. He knew that talking about it later would cost him money. He was beginning to be sorry he'd ever told the police about the holdups. He sighed now and said, 'It is three times in the past month.'

'Same guy each time?'

'*Two* of them. I don't know if it's the same. They are wearing – *come si dice? Maschere.*'

'Masks?'

'*Sì*, masks.'

'Same masks each time?'

'No. Once it was stockings, another time black ones, the third time handkerchiefs.'

Parker bit into the apple again. 'Are they armed?' he asked.

'If they did not have guns, I would break their heads and throw them out on the sidewalk.'

'Handguns?' Parker asked.

'What?'

'Pistols?'

'Yes, yes, pistols.'

'Both of them armed, or just one?'

'Both.'

'What time do they usually come in?'

'Different times. The first time was early in the morning, when I just opened the store. The next time was at night, maybe six, six-thirty. The last time was around lunch, the store was very quiet.'

'Did they take anything but cash?'

'Only cash.'

'Well,' Parker said, and shrugged. 'Maybe they'll come back, who knows? If you don't mind, I'll just hang around, okay? You got a back room or something?'

'Behind the curtain,' Silvio said. 'But if they come back again, I am ready for them myself.'

'What do you mean?'

'I got a gun now.'

He walked behind the counter to the cash register, opened it, and removed from the drawer a ·32 Smith & Wesson.

'You need a permit for that, you know,' Parker said.

'I got one. A man gets held up three times, nobody argues about giving him a permit.'

'Carry or premises?'

'Premises.'

'You know how to use that thing?' Parker asked.

'I know how, yes.'

'I've got some advice for you,' Parker said. 'If those hoods come back, leave your gun in the drawer. Let *me* take care of any shooting needs to be done.'

A woman was coming into the store. Without answering, Silvio turned away from Parker, smiled, and said to her, '*Buon giorno, signora.*'

Parker sighed, threw the curtain back, and went into the other room.

*   *   *

'What do you think?' Willis asked the assistant medical examiner.

'Fell or was pushed from someplace up there,' the ME said. 'Split his skull wide open when he hit the ground. Probably died on impact.'

'Anything else?'

'What more do you want? You're lucky we haven't got an omelette here.' He snapped his bag shut, rose from where he was crouched beside the body, and said, 'I'm finished, you can do what you like with him.'

'Thanks, Al,' Willis said.

'Yeah,' the ME answered, and walked off.

The body was now lying on its back. Genero looked down at the open skull and turned away. Dennison, the building superintendent, walked over with his hands in the pockets of his bib overalls. He looked down at the boy's bloody face and nodded.

'That's the kid in 4C,' he said.

'What's his name?'

'Scott.'

'That the first name or the last?'

'The last. I got his first name written down someplace inside. I got all the tenants' names written down. You want me to look it up for you?'

'Would you please?'

'Sure,' Dennison said.

'Would that be 4C up there?' Willis asked. 'The apartment with the broken window?'

'That's it, all right,' Dennison said.

The telephone on Arthur Brown's desk was ringing. He lifted the receiver, tucked it between his shoulder and his ear, said, 'Eighty-seventh Squad, Detective Brown,' and then glanced towards the slatted rail divider, where a patrolman was leading a handcuffed prisoner into the squad-room.

'Is this a detective?' the woman on the telephone asked.

'Yes, ma'am, Detective Brown.'

'I want to report a missing person,' the woman said.

'Yes, ma'am, just one second, please.'

Brown opened his desk drawer, took out a block of wood to which was attached the key to the detention cage across the room, and flipped it to the patrolman, who missed the catch. The prisoner laughed. The patrolman picked up the key, led the prisoner to the cage, opened the grillwork door, and shoved him inside.

'Take it easy, man,' the prisoner warned.

The patrolman locked the cage door without answering him. Then he walked to Brown's desk and sat on the edge of it, tilting his peaked cap back on his forehead and lighting a cigarette. On the telephone, Brown was saying, 'Now, what's your name, please, ma'am?'

'Mary Ellingham. Mrs Donald Ellingham.'

'Would you spell that for me, please?'

'E-L-L...'

'Yep...'

'...I-N-G, H-A-M.'

'And your address, Mrs Ellingham?'

'742 North Trinity.'

'All right, who's missing, Mrs Ellingham?'

'My husband.'

'That his full name? Donald Ellingham?'

'Yes. Well, no. Donald *E.* Ellingham. For Edward.'

'Yes, ma'am. How long has he been gone?'

'He was gone a week this past Friday.'

'Has this ever happened before, Mrs Ellingham?'

'No. Never.'

'He's never been gone before? Never any unexplained absences?'

'Never.'

'And you say he's been missing since, let's see, that'd be Friday the ninth?'

'Yes.'

'Did he go to work on Monday morning? The twelfth?'

'No.'

'You called his office?'

'Yes, I did.'

'And he wasn't there.'

'He hasn't been there all week.'

'Why'd you wait till today to report this, Mrs Ellingham?'

'I wanted to give him a chance to come back. I kept extending the deadline, you see. I thought I'd give him a few days, and then it turned into a week, and then I thought I'd give him just another day, and then Saturday went by, and . . . well, I decided to call today.'

'Does your husband drink, Mrs Ellingham?'

'No. That is, he drinks, but not excessively. He's not an alcoholic, if that's what you mean.'

'Has there ever been any problem with . . . well . . . other women?'

'No.'

'What I'm trying to say, Mrs Ellingham . . .'

'Yes, I understand. I don't think he's run off with another woman, no.'

'What *do* you think has happened, Mrs Ellingham?'

'I'm afraid he's been in an accident.'

'Have you contacted the various hospitals in the city?'

'Yes. He's not at any of them.'

'But you still think he may have been in an accident.'

'I think he may be dead someplace,' Mrs Ellingham said, and began weeping.

Brown was silent. He looked up at the patrolman.

'Mrs Ellingham?'

'Yes.'

'I'll try to get over there later today if I can, to get the information I'll need for the Missing Persons Bureau. Will you be home?'

'Yes.'

'Shall I call first?'

'No, I'll be here all day.'

'Fine, I'll see you later then. If you should hear anything meanwhile . . .'

'Yes, I'll call you.'

'Goodbye, Mrs Ellingham,' Brown said, and hung up.

'Lady's husband disappeared,' he said to the patrolman.

'Went down for a loaf of bread a year ago, right?' the patrolman said.

'Right. Hasn't been heard from since.' Brown gestured towards the detention cage. 'Who's the prize across the room?'

'Caught him cold in the middle of a burglary on Fifth and Friedlander. On a third-floor fire escape. Jimmied open the window, and was just entering.'

'Any tools on him?'

'Yep. I left them on the bench outside.'

'Want to get them for me?'

The patrolman went out into the corridor. Brown walked over to the detention cage. The prisoner looked at him.

'What's your name?' Brown asked.

'What's yours?'

'Detective Arthur Brown.'

'That's appropriate,' the prisoner said.

'I find it so,' Brown said coolly. 'Now what's yours?'

'Frederick Spaeth.'

The patrolman came back into the room carrying a leather bag containing a hand drill and bits of various sizes, a jimmy, a complete set of picklocks, several punches and skeleton keys, a pair of nippers, a hacksaw, a pair of brown cotton gloves, and a crowbar designed so that it could be taken apart and carried in three sections. Brown looked over the tools and said nothing.

'I'm a carpenter,' Spaeth said in explanation.

Brown turned to the patrolman. 'Anybody in the apartment, Simms?'

'Empty,' Simms replied.

'Spaeth,' Brown said, 'we're charging you with burglary in the third degree, which is a felony. And we're also charging you with Possession of Burglar's Instruments, which is a Class-A Misdemeanour. Take him down, Simms.'

'I want a lawyer,' Spaeth said.

'You're entitled to one,' Brown said.

'I want him *now*. Before you book me.'

Because policemen are sometimes as confused by Miranda-Escobedo as are laymen, Brown might have followed the course pursued by his colleague Kling, who, the night before, had advised a prisoner of his rights even though cruising radio patrolmen had arrested him in the act. Instead, Brown said, 'What for, Spaeth? You were apprehended entering an apartment illegally. Nobody's asking you any questions, we caught you cold. You'll be allowed three telephone calls after you're booked, to your lawyer, your mother, your bail bondsman, your best friend, whoever the hell you like. Take him down, Simms.'

Simms unlocked the cage and prodded Spaeth out of it with his nightstick. 'This is illegal!' Spaeth shouted.

'So's breaking and entering,' Brown answered.

The woman in the apartment across the hall from 4C was taller than both Willis and Genero, which was understandable. Hal Willis was the shortest man on the squad, having cleared the minimum five-feet-eight-inch height requirement by a scant quarter of an inch. Built like a soft shoe dancer, brown-haired and brown-eyed, he stood alongside Genero, who towered over him at five feet nine inches. Hal Willis knew he was short. Richard Genero thought he was very tall. From his father, he had inherited beautiful curly black hair and a strong Neapolitan nose, a sensuous mouth and soulful brown eyes. From his mother, he had inherited the tall Milanese carriage of all his male cousins and uncles – except Uncle Dominick, who was only five feet six. But this lady who opened the door to apartment 4B was a very big lady indeed. Both Willis and Genero looked up at her simultaneously, and then glanced at each other in something like stupefied awe. The lady was wearing a pink slip and nothing else. Barefooted, big-breasted, redheaded, green-eyed, she put her hands on her nylon-sheathed hips and said, 'Yeah?'

'Police officers,' Willis said, and showed her his shield.

The woman scrutinized it, and then said, 'Yeah?'

'We'd like to ask you a few questions,' Genero said.

'What about?'

'About the young man across the hall. Lewis Scott.'

'What about him?'

'Do you know him?'

'Slightly.'

'Only slightly?' Genero said. 'You live directly across the hall from him . . .'

'So what? This is the city.'

'Even so . . .'

'I'm forty-six years old, he's a kid of what? Eighteen? Nineteen? How do you *expect* me to know him? Intimately?'

'Well, no, ma'am, but . . .'

'So that's how I know him. Slightly. Anyway, what about him?'

'Did you see him at any time last night?' Willis asked.

'No. Why? Something happen to him?'

'Did you hear anything unusual in his apartment any time last night?'

'Unusual like what?'

'Like glass breaking?'

'I wasn't home last night. I went out to supper with a friend.'

'What time was that?'

'Eight o'clock.'

'And what time did you get back?'

'I didn't. I slept over.'

'With your friend?'

'Yes.'

'What's her name?' Genero asked.

'Her name is Morris Strauss, *that*'s her name.'

'Oh,' Genero said. He glanced at Willis sheepishly.

'When *did* you get home, ma'am?' Willis asked.

'About five o'clock this morning. Morris is a milkman. He gets up very early. We had breakfast together, and then I came back here. Why? What's the matter? Did Lew do something?'

'Did you happen to see him at *any* time yesterday?'

'Yeah. When I was going to the store. He was just coming in the building.'

'What time was that, would you remember?'

'About four-thirty. I was going out for some coffee. I ran out of coffee. I drink maybe six hundred cups of coffee a day. I'm always running out. So I was going up the street to the A&P to get some more. That's when I saw him.'

'Was he alone?'

'No.'

'Who was with him?'

'Another kid.'

'Boy or girl?'

'A boy.'

'Would you know who?' Genero asked.

'I don't hang around with teenagers, how would I . . .?'

'Well, you might have seen him around the neighbourhood . . .'

'No.'

'How old would you say he was?' Willis asked.

'About Lew's age. Eighteen, nineteen, I don't know. A big kid.'

'Can you describe him?'

'Long blond hair, a sort of handlebar moustache. He was wearing a crazy jacket.'

'What do you mean, crazy?'

'It was like an animal skin, with the fur inside and the, you know, what do you call it, the pelt? Is that what you call it?'

'Go ahead.'

'The raw side, you know what I mean? The skin part. That was the outside of the jacket, and the fur was the inside. White fur. And there was a big orange sun painted on the back of the jacket.'

'Anything else?'

'Ain't that enough?'

'Maybe it is,' Willis said. 'Thank you very much, ma'am.'

'You're welcome,' she answered. 'You want some coffee? I got some on the stove.'

'No, thanks, we want to take a look at the apartment here,' Genero said. 'Thanks a lot, though. You've been very kind.'

The woman smiled so suddenly and so radiantly that it almost knocked Genero clear across the hallway to the opposite wall.

'Not at all,' she said in a tiny little voice, and gently eased the door shut. Genero raised his eyebrows. He was trying to remember exactly what he had said, and in what tone of voice. He was still new at this business of questioning people, and any trick he could learn might prove helpful. The trouble was, he couldn't remember his exact words.

'What did I say?' he asked Willis.

'I don't remember,' Willis answered.

'No, come on, Hal, what did I say? What made her smile that way, and all of a sudden get so nice?'

'I think you asked her if she'd like to go to bed with you,' Willis said.

'No,' Genero said seriously, and shook his head. 'No, I don't think so.'

With the passkey the superintendent had provided, Willis opened the door to 4C, and stepped into the apartment. Behind him, Genero was still pondering the subtleties of police interrogation.

There were two windows facing the entrance door. The lower pane of the window on the left was almost completely shattered, with here and there an isolated shard jutting from the window frame. Sunlight streamed through both windows, dust motes rising silently. The apartment was sparsely furnished, a mattress on the floor against one wall, a bookcase on the opposite wall, a stereo record player and a stack of LP albums beside it, a bridge table and two chairs in the kitchen alcove, where another window opened on to the fire escape. A black camp trunk studded with brass rivets served as a coffee table in the centre of the room, near the record player. Brightly coloured cushions lined the wall on either side of the bookcase. Two black-and-white anti-war posters decorated the walls. The windows were curtainless. In the kitchen alcove, the shelves over the stove carried only two boxes of breakfast cereal and a bowl of sugar. A bottle of milk and three containers of yogurt were in the refrigerator. In the vegetable tray, Willis found a plastic bag of what looked like oregano. He showed it to Genero.

'Grass?' Genero said.

Willis shrugged. He opened the bag and sniffed the greenish-brown, crushed leaves. 'Maybe,' he said. He pulled an evidence tag from his pad, filled it out, and tied it to the plastic bag.

They went through the apartment methodically. There were three coffee mugs on the camp trunk. Each of them smelled of wine, and there was a red lipstick stain on the rim of one cup. They opened the camp trunk and found it stuffed with dungarees, flannel shirts, undershorts, several sweaters, a harmonica, an army blanket, and a small metal cash box. The cash box was unlocked. It contained three dollars in change, and a high school GO card encased in plastic. In the kitchen, they found two empty wine bottles in the garbage pail. A sprung mousetrap, the bait gone, was under the kitchen sink. On top of the closed toilet seat in the bathroom, they found a pair of dungarees with a black belt through the trouser loops, an orange Charlie Brown sweatshirt with the sleeves cut off raggedly at the elbows, a pair of white sweat socks, a pair of loafers and a woman's black silk blouse.

The blouse had a label in it.

They came into the grocery store at twenty minutes past seven, each of them wearing a Hallowe'en mask, even though this was only the middle of the month and Hallowe'en was still two weeks away. They were both holding drawn guns, both dressed in black trench coats and black trousers. They walked rapidly from the front door to the counter, with the familiarity of visitors who had been there before. One of them was wearing a Wolf Man mask and the other was wearing a Snow White mask. The masks completely covered their faces and lent a terrifying nightmare aspect to their headlong rush for the counter.

Silvio's back was turned when they entered the store. He heard the bell over the door, and whirled quickly, but they were almost to the counter by then, and he had time to shout only the single word '*Ancora!*' before he punched the NO SALE key on the register and reached into the drawer for his gun. The man wearing the Snow White mask was the first to realize that Silvio was going for a gun. He did not say a word to his partner. Instead, he fired directly into Silvio's face at close range. The slug almost tore off Silvio's head and sent him spinning backwards against the shelves. Canned goods clattered to the floor. The curtain leading to the back room was suddenly thrown open and Parker stood in the doorway with a ·38 Police Special in his fist. The man with the Wolf Man mask had his hand in the cash drawer and was scooping up a pile of bills.

'Hold it!' Parker shouted, and the man with the Snow White mask fired again. His slug caught Parker in the right shoulder. Parker bent low and pulled off a wild shot just as the man at the cash register opened fire, aiming for Parker's belly, catching him in the leg instead. Parker grabbed for the curtain behind him, clutching for support, tearing it loose as he fell to the floor screaming in pain.

The two men in their Hallowe'en masks ran out of the store and into the Sunday morning sunshine.

There were 186 patrolmen assigned to the 87th Precinct and on any given day of the week, their work schedule was outlined by a duty chart that required a PhD in Arabic literature to be properly understood. In essence, six of these patrolmen worked from 8 AM to 4 PM, Monday to Friday, two of them serving as the Captain's clerical force, one as a highway safety patrolman, and the last two as community relations patrolman and roll call man respectively. The remaining 180 patrolmen were divided into twenty squads with nine men on each squad. Their duty chart looked like this:

SCHEDULE OF DUTY FOR PATROLMEN ‡

JAN.	FEB.	MAR.	APR.	MAY	JUNE	JULY	AUG.	SEPT.	OCT.	NOV.	DEC.	12 MID. TO 8 A.M. SQUAD	8 A.M. TO 4 P.M. SQUAD	4 P.M. TO 12 MID. SQUAD	DAY ON CHART
3-23	12	4-24	(13)	(3)-23	12	2-22	11-(31)	(20)	10-30	19	9-29	(1)2-3-4-5	8-9-10-11-12	15-16-17-18-19	1
(4)-24	13	5-25	14	(4)-24	13	3-23	12	1-(21)	(11)-31	20	10-30	2-3-4-5-6	9-10-11-12-13	16-17-18-19-20	2
(5)-25	14	6-26	15	5-25	(14)	4-24	13	2-22	(12)	(21)	11-31	3-4-5-6-7	10-11-12-13-14	17-18-19-20-1	3
6-26	(15)	7-27	16	6-26	(15)	(5)-25	14	3-23	13	(22)	12	4-5-6-7-8	11-12-13-14-15	18-19-20-1-2	4
7-27	(16)	8-28	17	7-27	16	(6)-26	15	4-24	14	(23)	(13)	5-6-7-8-9	12-13-14-15-16	19-20-1-2-3	5
8-28	17	(8)-29	18	8-28	17	7-(27)	(16)	5-25	15	4-24	(14)	6-7-8-9-10	13-14-15-16-17	20-1-2-3-4	6
9-29	18	(9)-29	(19)	9-29	18	8-28	(17)	6-26	16	5-25	15	7-8-9-10-11	14-15-16-17-18	1-2-3-4-5	7
10-30	19	10-30	(20)	(9)-30	19	9-29	18	6-(27)	17	6-26	16	8-9-10-11-12	15-16-17-18-19	2-3-4-5-6	8
(11)-31	20	11-31	1-21	(10)-30	20	9-29	19	7-(27)	(18)	7-27	17	9-10-11-12-13	16-17-18-19-20	3-4-5-6-7	9
12	1-21	12	2-22	(11)-31	(1)-21	11-31	20	8-(28)	(19)	8-28	18	10-11-12-13-14	17-18-19-20-1	4-5-6-7-8	10
13	(22)	13	3-23	12	2-22	(12)	1-21	9-29	20	9-(29)	19	11-12-13-14-15	18-19-20-1-2	5-6-7-8-9	11
14	(23)	14	4-24	13	3-23	(13)	2-22	10-30	1-21	10-(30)	20	12-13-14-15-16	19-20-1-2-3	6-7-8-9-10	12
15	3	(15)	5-25	14	4-24	14	(23)	11	2-22	11	(21)	13-14-15-16-17	20-1-2-3-4	7-8-9-10-11	13
16	4-24	(16)	6-26	15	5-25	15	(24)	12	10-30	12	(22)	14-15-16-17-18	1-2-3-4-5	8-9-10-11-12	14
17	5-25	17	7-27	16	6-26	16	4-24	13	1-21	10-30	(23)	15-16-17-18-19	2-3-4-5-6	9-10-11-12-13	15
18	6-26	18	8-28	17	7-27	17	5-25	14	2-22	11	4-24	16-17-18-19-20	3-4-5-6-7	10-11-12-13-14	16
19	7-27	19	9-29	(17)	8-28	18	6-26	15	6-(26)	12	5-25	17-18-19-20-1	4-5-6-7-8	11-12-13-14-15	17
(19)	(8)-28	20	1-21	18	(8)-29	(19)	7-27	16	7-27	13	6-26	18-19-20-1-2	5-6-7-8-9	12-13-14-15-16	18
1-21	9	(21)	11	20	(9)-29	(20)	8-28	17	8-28	17	7-(27)	19-20-1-2-3	6-7-8-9	13-14-15-16-17	19
2-22	10	(22)	(12)	2-22	11	1-21	9-(30)	18	9-29	18	8-(28)	20-1-2-3-4	7-8-9-10-11	14-15-16-17-18	20

1969 — TOURS OF DUTY

○ AROUND SQUAD NUMBER INDICATES EXCUSAL EXCEPT WHEN IT CORRESPONDS WITH ○ AROUND DATE

○ INDICATES SATURDAYS & SUNDAYS

‡ TO BE USED BY: PATROL PRECINCTS, EMERGENCY SERVICE, ACCIDENT INVESTIGATION SQUAD, SGTS & PTL OF HARBOR PCT.

EFF. 1-1-66

All of which meant that patrolmen worked five tours for a forty-hour week, and then were off for fifty-six hours except when they were working the midnight to 8 AM shift, in which case they then worked only *four* tours and were off for eighty hours. Unless, of course, the *fifth* midnight tour happened to fall on a Friday or Saturday night, in which case they were required to work. All clear?

Patrolmen were supposed to be relieved on post as soon as possible after the hour by the squad that had just answered roll call in the precinct muster room. But most patrolmen began to drift back towards the station house shortly before the hour, so that seconds after the new shift trotted down the precinct steps, the old one entered the building and headed for the locker room to change into street clothes. There were a lot of cops in and around a police station when the shift was changing, and Sunday morning was no exception. If anything, the precinct was busier on Sunday because Saturday night brought thieves out like cockroaches and their resultant handiwork spilled over on to the day of rest.

This particular Sunday morning was more chaotic than usual because a cop had been shot, and nothing can galvanize a police department like the knowledge that one of their own has been gunned down. Lieutenant Peter Byrnes, who was in command of the sixteen detectives on the 87th Squad, saw fit to call in three men who were on vacation, perhaps on the theory that one wounded cop is worth at least three who were ambulatory. Not content to leave it at that, he then put in a call to Steve Carella at his home in Riverhead, ostensibly to inform him of the shooting.

Sitting behind his desk in the corner room upstairs, looking down at the front steps of the building, where the patrolmen filed out in pairs, the green globes flanking the steps and burning with sunshine as though fired from within, Byrnes must have known that Carella had worked the night shift and that the man did not now need a call from his superior officer. But he dialled the number none the less, and waited while the phone rang repeatedly on the

other end. When at last Carella answered, Byrnes said,
'Steve? Were you asleep?'

'No, I was just getting into my pyjamas.'

'Sorry to bother you this way.'

'No, no, what is it, Pete?'

'Parker just got shot in a grocery store on Ainsley.'

'No kidding?'

'Yeah.'

'Jesus,' Carella said.

'Two hoods killed the proprietor, wounded Parker in the
shoulder and leg. He's been taken to Buenavista Hospital.
It looks pretty serious.'

'Jesus,' Carella said again.

'I've already called in Di Maeo, Levine, and Meriwether.
They're on vacation, Steve, but I *had* to do it, I don't like it
when cops get shot.'

'No, neither do I.'

'I just thought I'd tell you.'

'Yeah, I'm glad you did, Pete.'

The line went silent.

'Pete?'

'Yeah, Steve?'

'What is it? Do you want *me* to come in, too?'

'Well, you had a long night, Steve.'

The line was silent again.

'Well . . . what do you want me to do, Pete?'

'Why don't you see how you feel?' Byrnes said. 'Go to bed,
get some rest, maybe you'll feel like coming in a little later,
okay?' Byrnes paused. 'I can use you, Steve. It's up to you.'

'What time is it, anyway?' Carella asked.

Byrnes looked up at the wall clock. 'Little after eight. Get
some rest, okay?'

'Yeah, okay,' Carella said.

'I'll talk to you later,' Byrnes said, and hung up. He rose
from behind his desk, hooked his thumbs into his belt just
above both hip pockets and walked to the window overlooking the park. He was a compact man with grey hair and
flinty blue eyes, and he stood looking silently at the sun-

washed foliage across the street, his face expressionless, and
then turned suddenly and walked to the frosted glass door of
his office, yanked it open, and went out into the squad-
room.

A marine corporal was sitting with Detective Carl Kapek
at the desk closest to the lieutenant's office. A swollen dis-
coloured lump the size of a baseball sat just over the
marine's left eye. His uniform was rumpled and soiled, and
he looked extremely embarrassed, his hands clasped in his
lap rather like a schoolboy's. He spoke in a very low voice,
almost a whisper, to Kapek as the lieutenant walked past
them to where Brown was on the telephone at his own desk.

'Right, I'll tell him,' Brown said, and replaced the phone
on its cradle.

'That about Parker?' Byrnes asked.

'No, that was Delgado over on South Sixth. Guy was on his
way to church, four other guys grabbed him as he came out
of his building, damn near killed him. Delgado's on it
now.'

'Right. The hospital call back on Parker?'

'Not yet.'

'Who's that in the holding cell downstairs?'

'A burglar Simms picked up on Fifth and Friedlander.'

'You'd better get over to that grocery store, Artie.'

'That'll leave Kapek all alone here.'

'I've got some men coming in. They should be here anytime now.'

'Okay then.'

'I want some meat on this, Artie. I don't like my squad
getting shot up.'

Brown nodded, opened the top drawer of his desk, and
took from it a holstered ·38 Detective's Special. He fastened
the holster to his belt just slightly forward of his right hip
pocket, put on his jacket, and then went to the locker room
to get his coat and hat. On his way out of the squad-room, he
stopped at Kapek's desk and said, 'I'll be at that grocery
store, if you need me.'

'Okay,' Kapek said, and turned back to the marine. 'I still

don't understand exactly how you got beat up,' he said. 'You mind going over it one more time?'

The marine looked even more embarrassed now. He was short and slender, dwarfed by Kapek, who sat beside him in his shirt sleeves with his tie pulled down, collar open, straight blond hair falling onto his forehead, wearing a shoulder holster from which protruded the walnut butt of a ·38.

'Well, you know, I got jumped, is all,' the marine said.

'How?'

'I was walking along, and I got jumped, is all.'

'Where was this, Corporal Miles?'

'On The Stem.'

'What time?'

'Must've been about three in the morning.'

'What were you doing?'

'Just walking.'

'Going any place in particular?'

'I'd just left this bar, you see? I'd been drinking in this bar on Seventeenth Street, I think it was.'

'Anything happen in the bar?'

'Well, like what?'

'Any trouble? Any words?'

'No, no, it was a real nice bar.'

'And you left there about three o'clock and started walking up The Stem.'

'That's right.'

'Where were you going?'

'Oh, just for a little walk, that's all. Before heading back to the ship. I'm on this battleship over to the Navy Yard. It's in dry dock there.'

'Um-huh,' Kapek said. 'So you were walking along and this man jumped you.'

'Mmm.'

'Just one man?'

'Yeah. One.'

'What'd he hit you with?'

'I don't know.'

'And you came to just a little while ago, is that it?'

'Yeah. And found out the bastards had taken my wallet and watch.'

Kapek was silent for several seconds. Then he said, 'I thought there was only one of them.'

'That's right. Just one.'

'You said "bastards".'

'Huh?'

'Plural.'

'Huh?'

'How many were there actually, Corporal?'

'Who hit me, you mean? Like I said. Just one.'

'Never mind who hit you or who didn't. How many were there altogether?'

'Well ... two.'

'All right, let's get this straight now. It was *two* men who jumped you, not ...'

'Well, no. Not exactly.'

'Look, Corporal,' Kapek said, 'you want to tell me about this, or you want to forget it? We're pretty busy around here right now, and I don't have time for this kind of thing, I mean. You want us to try to recover your stuff, then give us a little help, okay? Otherwise, so long, it was nice meeting you, I hope you get back to your ship all right.'

Miles was silent for several moments. Then he sighed deeply, and said, 'I feel like a goddamn jackass, is all.'

'Why? What happened?'

'There was this girl in the bar ...'

'I figured,' Kapek said, and nodded.

'In a red dress. She kept wiggling her ass at me all night long, you know? So I finally started a conversation with her, and she was real friendly and all, I mean she didn't seem to be *after* nothing, I think I maybe bought her only two drinks the whole night long.'

'Yeah, go ahead.'

'So a little before three, she tells me she's awful tired and wants to go home to bed, and she says goodnight to every-body, and then goes to the door and winks at me and gives me a kind of a little come-on move with her head, you know? Like this, you know? Like just this little movement of her head, you know? To tell me I should follow her. So I paid the bill, and hurried on outside, and there she was on the corner, and she starts walking the minute she sees me, looking back over her shoulder, and giving me that same come-on again, trotting her little ass right up the avenue, and then turning off into one of the side streets. So I turned the corner after her and there's this guy standing there, and wham, he clobbers me. Next thing I know, I wake up with *this* fucking thing over my eye, and my money gone, and my watch, too. Little bitch.'

'Was she black or white?'

'Black.'

'And the man?'

'White.'

'Would you recognize her if you saw her again?'

'I'll never forget her long as I live.'

'What about the man?'

'I only got a quick look at him. He hit me the minute I come around that corner. Man, I saw stars. They musta moved me after I went out because I woke up in this hallway, you see. I mean, I was laying on the sidewalk when . . .' Miles stopped and looked down at his hands.

'Yes, Corporal?'

'What gets me is, I mean, she *kicked* me, the little bitch. When I was down on the sidewalk, she kicked me with this goddamn pointed shoe of hers. I mean, man, *that's* what put me out, not the guy hitting me. It was her kicking me with that pointed shoe of hers.' Corporal Miles looked up plaintively. 'Why'd she do *that*, huh? I was nice to her. I mean it. I was only nice.'

The ambulance had come and gone, carrying away the man who had been attacked as he was leaving his home to go to church. It was now nine o'clock and there was still blood on the front stoop of the building. Detective/3rd Grade Alexandre Delgado stood on the steps with the victim's wife and two children, and tried to believe they were unaware of the blood drying in the early morning sunshine. Mrs Huerta was a black-haired woman with brown eyes filled now with tears. Her two daughters, dressed to go to church, wearing identical green wool coats and black patent leather shoes and white ankle socks, resembled their mother except for the tears. Their brown eyes were opened wide in curiosity and fright and incomprehension. But neither of the two was crying. A crowd of bystanders kept nudging towards the stoop, despite the efforts of the beat patrolman to disperse them.

'Can you tell me exactly what happened, Mrs Huerta?' Delgado asked. Like the woman he was questioning, he was Puerto Rican. And like her, he had been raised in a ghetto. Not this one, but a similar one (when you've seen *one* slum, you've seen them all, according to certain observers) in the shadow of the Calm's Point Bridge downtown. He could have spoken to her in fluent Spanish, but he was still slightly embarrassed by his accent when he was speaking English, and as a result he tried to speak it *all* the time. Mrs Huerta, on the other hand, was not so sure she wanted to conduct the conversation in English. Her young daughters understood and spoke English, whereas their Spanish was spotty at best. At the same time, many of Mrs Huerta's neighbours (who were eagerly crowding the front stoop now) spoke *only* Spanish, and she recognized that talking to this detective in English might enable her to keep at least some of her business to herself. She silently debated the matter only a moment longer, and then decided to answer in English.

'We were going down to church,' she said, 'the eight o'clock mass. The church is right up the street, it takes five minutes. We came out of the building, José and me and the two girls, and these men came at him.'

'How many men?'

'Four.'

'Did you recognize any of them?'

'No,' Mrs Huerta said.

'What happened?'

'They hit him.'

'With what?'

'Broom handles. Short. You know, they take the broom and saw it off.'

'Did they say anything to your husband?'

'*Nada*. Nothing.'

'Did he say anything to them?'

'No.'

'And you didn't recognize any of them? They weren't men from the *barrio*, the neighbourhood?'

'I never saw them before.'

One of the little girls looked up at her mother and then turned quickly away.

'*Sí, qué hay?*' Delgado asked immediately.

'Nothing,' the little girl answered.

'What's your name?' Delgado said.

'Paquita Huerta.'

'Did you see the men who attacked your father, Paquita?'

'Yes,' Paquita said, and nodded.

'Did you know any of those men?'

The little girl hesitated.

'*Puede usted decirme?*'

'No,' Paquita said. 'I did not know any of them.'

'And you?' Delgado said, turning to the other girl.

'No. None of them.'

Delgado searched their eyes. The little girls watched him unblinkingly. He turned to Mrs Huerta again. 'Your husband's full name is José Huerta?' he asked.

'José Vicente Huerta.'

'How old is he, *señora*?'

'Forty-seven.'

'What does he do for a living?'

'He is a real estate agent.'

'Where is his place of business, Mrs Huerta?'

'In Riverhead. 1345 Harrison Avenue. It is called J-R Realty.'

'Does he own the business?'

'Yes.'

'No partners?'

'Yes, he has a partner.'

'What's his partner's name?'

'Ramon Castañeda. That's how they got the J-R. From José and Ramon.'

'And where does Mr Castañeda live?'

'Two blocks from here. On Fourth Street.'

'The address?'

'112 South Fourth.'

'All right, thank you,' Delgado said. 'I'll let you know if we come up with anything.'

'*Por favor*,' Mrs Huerta said, and took both her daughters by their hands and led them into the building.

The black blouse found in Lewis Scott's bathroom had come from a clothing store called the Monkey Wrench, on Culver Avenue. Since this was a Sunday, the store was closed. The patrolman on the beat spotted Willis and Genero peering through the plate-glass window and casually ambled over to them.

'Help you fellows?' he asked.

Both Genero and Willis looked at him. Neither of them recognized him. 'You new on the beat, kid?' Genero said. The patrolman was perhaps three or four years *older* than Genero, but since his rank was lower, Genero felt perfectly free to address him in this manner. The patrolman could not decide whether he was dealing with hoods or fellow law enforcers; the distinction was sometimes difficult to make. He debated whether he should answer smart-ass or subservient. While he was deciding, Willis said, 'I'm Detective Willis. This is my partner, Detective Genero.'

'Oh,' the patrolman said, managing to make the single word sound eloquent.

'How long you been on the beat, kid?' Genero asked.

'Just this past week. They flew me in from Majesta.'

'Special assignment?'

'Yeah. This is a glass post, you know, there's been lots of

breakage and looting lately. They almost doubled the force here, from what I understand.'

'Where's the regular beat man?'

'He's catching a cup of coffee at the diner up the street. Anything I can help you with?'

'What's his name?'

'Haskins. You know him?'

'Yeah,' Willis said. 'Diner on the corner there?'

'Right.'

'See you later, kid,' Genero said, and both detectives walked off towards the diner. Behind them, the patrolman shrugged in a manner clearly indicating that he thought all detectives were no-good rotten bastards who were always pulling rank.

The diner at fifteen minutes before ten was empty save for Patrolman Haskins and a man behind the counter. Haskins was hunched over a cup of coffee. He looked as though he had not had much sleep the night before. Genero and Willis walked to the counter and took stools on either side of him.

'Hello, Bill,' Willis said.

Haskins looked up from his coffee. 'Hey, hi,' he said.

'Two coffees,' Genero said to the counterman.

'You looking for me,' Haskins asked, 'or you just happen in?'

'We're looking for you.'

'What's up?'

'How you want those coffees?' the counterman asked.

'Regular,' Willis said.

'One regular, one black,' Genero said.

'Two regulars, one black,' the counterman said.

'*One* regular, *one* black,' Genero said.

'*He* wants a regular,' the counterman insisted, 'and *you* want a regular and a black.'

'What are you, a comedian?' Genero said.

'It's all on the arm anyway, ain't it?' the counterman answered.

'Who says?'

'The day a cop pays for a cup of coffee in here, that's the day they give me a parade up Hall Avenue.'

None of the policemen answered him. They were not, as a matter of fact, in the habit of paying for coffee in local eateries. Neither did they enjoy being reminded of it.

'Bill, we're looking for a kid about eighteen, nineteen,' Willis said. 'Long blond hair; handlebar moustache. See anybody around like that?'

'I seen a hundred of them,' Haskins said. 'Are you kidding?'

'This one was wearing a jacket with the fur side inside, the skin side out.'

Haskins shrugged.

'Big sun painted on the back of it,' Willis said.

'Yeah, that rings a bell. I think I seen that jacket around.'

'Remember the kid wearing it?'

'Where the hell did I see that jacket?' Haskins asked aloud.

'He might have been with another kid his age, black beard, black hair.'

'No,' Haskins said, and shook his head. 'An orange sun, right? Like an orange sun with rays coming out of it, right?'

'That's right, orange.'

'Yeah, I seen that jacket,' Haskins said. 'Just the other day. Where the hell did I see it?'

'Two coffees, one regular, one black,' the counterman said, and put them down.

'Jerry, you ever see a kid in here wearing a fur jacket with a sun painted on the back of it?' Haskins asked.

'No,' the counterman said flatly, and walked back into the kitchen.

'White fur, right?' Haskins said to Willis. 'On the inside, right? Like white fur?'

'That's right.'

'Sure, I seen that goddamn jacket. Just give me a minute, okay?'

'Sure, take your time,' Willis said.

Haskins turned to Genero and conversationally said, 'I see you got the gold tin. Who's your rabbi?'

'I was promoted a long time ago,' Genero said, somewhat offended. 'Where the hell have you been?'

'I guess I don't keep up with what's happening around the station house,' Haskins said, and grinned.

'You *know* I was promoted.'

'Yeah, I guess it just slipped my mind,' Haskins said. 'How you like the good life, Genero?'

'Beats laying bricks all to hell,' Genero answered.

'What *doesn't*?' Haskins said.

'About that jacket . . .' Willis interrupted.

'Yeah, yeah, just give me a minute it'll come to me,' Haskins, said, and lifted his coffee cup in both hands, and sipped at it and said, 'That new kid covering out there?'

'He's doing fine, don't worry about him.'

'The Monkey Wrench!' Haskins said, snapping his fingers. '*That's* where I seen the damn thing. In the window of the Monkey Wrench. Right up the street.'

'Good,' Willis said, and nodded. 'Got any ideas who runs that shop?'

'Yeah, these two dykes who live over on Eighth. Just around the corner from the store.'

'What're their names?'

'Flora Schneider and Frieda something. I don't know what. Flora and Frieda, everybody calls them.'

'What's the address on Eighth?'

'327 North. The brownstone right around the corner.'

'Thanks,' Willis said.

'Thanks for the coffee,' Genero yelled to the kitchen.

The counterman did not answer.

Detective Arthur Brown was a black man with a very dark complexion, kinky hair, large nostrils, and thick lips. He was impressively good looking, though unfortunately not cast in the Negro mould acceptable to most white people, including liberals. In short, he did not resemble Harry Belafonte, Sidney Poitier, or Adam Clayton Powell. He resembled only himself, which was quite a lot since he was six feet four inches tall and weighed two hundred and twenty pounds. Arthur Brown was the sort of black man who caused white men to cross the street when he approached, on the theory that this mean-looking son of a bitch (mean-looking only because he was big and black) would undoubtedly mug them or knife them or do something possibly worse, God knew what. Even after Brown identified himself as a police detective, there were many white people who still harboured the suspicion that he was really some kind of desperate criminal impersonating an officer.

It was therefore a pleasant surprise for Brown to come across a witness to the grocery store shootings who did not seem at all intimidated by either his size or his colour. The person was a little old lady who carried a bright blue umbrella on her arm, despite the fact that the day was clear, with that sharp penetrating bite in the air that comes only with October. The umbrella matched the lady's eyes, which were as clear and as sharp as the day itself. She wore a little flowered hat on her head. If she had been a younger woman, the black coat she was wearing might have been called a maxi. She leaped to her feet as Brown came through the front door of the grocery, and said to him in a brisk resonant voice, 'Ah, at last!'

'Ma'am?' Brown said.

'You're the detective, aren't you?'

'I am,' Brown admitted.

'My name is Mrs Farraday, how do you do?'

'Detective Brown,' he said, and nodded, and would have let it go at that, but Mrs Farraday was holding out her hand. Brown clasped it, shook it, and smiled pleasantly. Mrs Farraday returned the smile and released his hand.

'They told me to wait in here, said a detective would be along any minute. I've been waiting half the morning. It's past ten-thirty now.'

'Well, Mrs Farraday, I've been talking to people in the

neighbourhood since a little after eight o'clock. Takes a little while to get around to all of them.'

'Oh, I can well imagine,' she said.

'Patrolman outside says you've got some information for me, though. Is that right?'

'That's right. I saw the two men who held up the store.'

'Where'd you see them?'

'Running around the corner. I was on my way home from church, I always go to six o'clock mass, and I'm generally out by seven, and then I stop at the bakery for buns, my husband likes buns with his breakfast on Sundays, or coffee cake.'

'Um-huh.'

'Never goes to church himself,' she said, 'damn heathen.'

'Um-huh.'

'I was coming out of the bakery – this must have been, oh, close to seven-thirty – when I saw the two of them come running around the corner. I thought at first . . .'

'What were they wearing, Mrs Farraday?'

'Black coats. And masks. One of them was a girl's face – the mask, I mean. And the other was a monster mask, I don't know which monster. They had guns. Both of them. But none of that's important, Detective Brown.'

'What *is* important?'

'They took the masks *off*. As soon as they turned the corner, they took the masks off, and I got a very good look at both of them.'

'Can you describe them to me now?'

'I certainly can.'

'Good.' Brown took out his pad and flipped it open. He reached into his pocket for his pen – he was one of the few cops on the squad who still used a fountain pen rather than a ball-point – took off the cap, and said, 'Were they white or black, Mrs Farraday?'

'White,' Mrs Farraday said.

'How old would you say they were?'

'Young.'

'How young? Twenty? Thirty?'

'Oh, no. In their forties, I would say. They were young, but they were definitely not *kids*, Detective Brown.'

'How tall were they?'

'One was about your height, a very big man. How tall are you?'

'Six four,' Brown said.

'My that *is* big,' Mrs Farraday said.

'And the other one?'

'Much shorter. Five eight or nine, I would guess.'

'Notice the hair colour?'

'The short one was blond. The tall one had dark hair.'

'I don't suppose you saw the colour of their eyes.'

'They passed close enough, but I just didn't see. They went by very quickly.'

'Any scars? Tattoos? Birthmarks?'

'Not that I could see.'

'Both clean-shaven?'

'Do you mean did they have beards or moustaches?'

'Yes, ma'am.'

'No, both clean-shaven.'

'You say they took the masks off as they came around the corner, is that right?'

'Yes. They just ripped them off. It must be difficult to see through those things, wouldn't you imagine?'

'Was there a car waiting for them?'

'No, I don't think they had a car, Detective Brown. They were running too fast for that. It's my guess they were trying to make their escape on foot. Wouldn't that be your guess as well?'

'I really couldn't say yet, Mrs Farraday. I wonder if you could show me where that bakery store is.'

'Certainly. It's right around the corner.'

They walked out of the grocery, and the patrolman outside said to Brown, 'You know anything about when I'm supposed to be relieved here?'

'What do you mean?' Brown asked.

'I think there's some kind of foul-up. I mean, this ain't even my post.'

'Where *is* your post?'

'On Grover Avenue. Near the park.'

'So what're you doing here?'

'That's just it. I collared this guy around quarter to seven, must've been, and took him back to the station house to book him – he was trying to bust into a Mercedes parked on South Second. By the time I got finished there, it was like seven-fifteen, and Nealy and O'Hara are going by in a patrol car, so I hail them and ask for a lift back to my post. We're on the way when all of a sudden they catch the radio squeal about the shooting here at the grocery store. So we all rush over here, and there's a big hullabaloo, you know, Parker caught some stuff, you know, and Nealy and O'Hara take off on a Ten-Thirteen, and the sergeant tells me to stay here outside the door. So I been here all morning. I was supposed to be relieved on post at eight o'clock, but how's my relief supposed to know where I am so he can relieve me? You going back to the station house?'

'Not right away.'

'Listen, I hate to leave here, because the sarge might get sore, you know? He told me to stay right here.'

'I'll call in from the nearest box,' Brown said.

'Would you do that? I certainly would appreciate it.'

'Right away,' Brown said.

He and Mrs Farraday walked around the corner to the bakery shop. 'This is where I was standing when they ran by,' Mrs Farraday said. 'They were taking off the masks as they came around the corner, and they had them off by the time they passed me. Then they went racing up the street there and ... oh, my goodness!' she said, and stopped.

'What is it, Mrs Farraday?'

'I just remembered what they did with those masks, Detective Brown. They threw them down the sewer there. They stopped at the sewer grating and just threw them away, and then they started running again.'

'Thank you, Mrs Farraday,' Brown said, 'you've been most helpful.'

'Oh, well,' she said, and smiled.

Flora and Frieda did not get back to their apartment on North Eighth until seven minutes past eleven. They were both pretty women in their late twenties, both wearing pants suits and short car coats. Flora was a blonde, Frieda a redhead. Flora wore big gold hoop earrings. Frieda had a tiny black beauty spot near the corner of her mouth. They explained to the detectives that they always walked in the park on Sunday mornings, rain or shine. Flora offered them tea, and when they accepted, Frieda went upstairs to the kitchen, to put the kettle on.

Their apartment was in a brownstone that had run the gamut from luxury dwelling fifty years back, to crumbling tenement for as many years, to reconverted town house in a block of similar buildings trying desperately to raise their heads above the slime of the neighbourhood. The women owned the entire building, and Flora explained now that the bedrooms were on the top floor, the kitchen, dining-room and spare room on the middle floor, and the living-room on the ground floor. The detectives were sitting with her in that room now, sunlight streaming through the damask-hung windows. A cat lay before the tiled fireplace, dozing. The living-room ran the entire length of the ground floor, and was warmly and beautifully furnished. There was a false sense here of being someplace other than the city – some English country home in Dorset perhaps, or some Welsh manor; quiet and secluded, with gently rolling grassy hills just outside the door. But it was one thing to convert a slum building into a beautiful town house, and quite another to ignore the whirlpool surrounding it. Neither Flora nor Frieda were fools; there were iron gates over the windows facing the backyard, and a Fox lock on the front door.

'The store hasn't been burgled, has it?' Flora asked. Her voice was somewhat throaty. She sounded very much like a torch singer holding the mike too close to her lips.

'No, no,' Willis assured her. 'We merely want to ask about some articles of clothing that may have been purchased there.'

'Thank heavens,' Flora said. Frieda had come down from the kitchen and stood now behind Flora's wingback chair, her hand delicately resting on the lace antimacassar just behind her partner's head.

'We've been burgled four times since we opened the store,' Frieda said.

'Each time they've taken, oh, less than a hundred dollars worth of merchandise. It's ridiculous. It costs us more to replace the broken glass each time. If they'd just come in the store and *ask* for the damn stuff, we'd give it to them outright.'

'We've had the locks changed four times, too. That all costs money,' Frieda said.

'We operate on a very low profit margin,' Flora said.

'It's junkies who do it,' Frieda said. 'Don't you think so, Flora?'

'Oh, no question,' Flora said. 'Hasn't that been your experience?' she asked the detectives.

'Well, sometimes,' Willis said. 'But not all burglars are junkies.'

'Are all junkies burglars?' Frieda asked.

'Some of them.'

'Most of them?'

'A lot of them. Takes quite a bit of money to support a habit, you know.'

'The city ought to do something about it,' Flora said.

The cat near the fireplace stirred, stretched, blinked at the detectives, and then stalked out of the room.

'Pussy's getting hungry,' Flora said.

'We'll feed her soon,' Frieda answered.

'What clothes did you want to ask about?' Flora said.

'Well, primarily a jacket you had in the window last week. A fur jacket with . . .'

'The llama, yes, what about it?'

'With an orange sun painted on the back?' Genero said.

'Yes, that's it.'

'Would you remember who you sold it to?' Willis asked.

'I didn't sell it,' Flora said. She glanced up at her partner. 'Frieda?'

'Yes, I sold it,' Frieda said.

'Would you remember who bought it?'

'A boy. Long blond hair and a moustache. A young boy. I explained to him that it was really a woman's coat, but he said that didn't matter, he thought it was groovy and wanted it. It has no buttons, you realize, so that wasn't any problem. A woman's garment buttons differently . . .'

'Yes, I know that.'

'This particular coat is held closed with a belt. I remember him trying it *with* the belt and then *without* the belt.'

'Excuse me,' Genero said, 'but is this a coat or a jacket?'

'Well, it's a short coat, actually. Mid-thigh. It's really designed for a woman, to go with a miniskirt. It's about that length.'

'I see.'

'I guess a man could wear it, though,' Frieda said dubiously.

'Do you know who the boy was?'

'I'm sorry, I don't. I'd never seen him before.'

'How much did the coat cost?'

'A hundred and ten dollars.'

'Did he pay for it in cash?'

'No, by . . . oh, of course.'

'Yes?' Willis said.

'He gave me a cheque. His name would be on the cheque, wouldn't it?' She turned to Flora. 'Where are the cheques we're holding for deposit tomorrow?' she asked.

'Upstairs,' Flora said. 'In the locked drawer.' She smiled at the detectives and said, 'One drawer in the dresser locks. Not that it would do any good if someone decided to break in here.'

'Shall I get it for you?' Frieda asked.

'If you would,' Willis said.

'Certainly. The tea must be ready, too.'

She went out of the room. Her tread sounded softly on the carpeted steps leading upstairs.

'There was one other item,' Willis said. 'Dick, have you got that blouse?'

Genero handed him a manila envelope. Willis unclasped it, and removed from it the black silk blouse they had found on Scott's bathroom floor, the police evidence tag dangling from one of its buttons. Flora took the blouse and turned it over in her hands.

'Yes, that's ours,' she said.

'Would you know who bought it from you?'

Flora shook her head. 'I really couldn't say. We sell dozens of blouses every week.' She looked at the label. 'This is a thirty-four, a very popular size.' She shook her head again. 'No, I'm sorry.'

'Okay,' Willis said. He put the blouse back into the envelope. Frieda was coming into the room with a tray upon which was a teapot covered with a cosy, four cups and saucers, a milk pitcher, a sugar bowl, and several sliced lemons in a low dish. A cheque was under the sugar bowl. Frieda put down the tray, lifted the sugar bowl and handed the cheque to Willis.

A name and an address were printed across the top of the cheque:

ROBERT HAMLING
3541 Carrier Avenue
Isola

The cheque was made out to the order of The Monkey Wrench for one hundred thirty-five dollars and sixty-eight cents; it was signed by Hamling in a broad, sprawling hand. Willis looked up. 'I thought the coat cost a hundred and ten dollars. This cheque . . .'

'Yes, he bought a blouse as well. The blouse cost eighteen dollars. The rest is tax.'

'A black silk blouse?' Genero asked.

'Yes,' Frieda said.

'*This* one?' Genero asked, and pulled the blouse from its

envelope like a magician pulling a rabbit from a hat.

'Yes, that's the blouse,' Frieda said.

Genero nodded in satisfaction. Willis turned the cheque over. On the back of it were the penned words: 'Drivers Lic' and the numbers '21546 68916 506607–52'.

'Did you write this?' Willis asked.

'Yes,' Frieda answered.

'He showed you identification, I take it.'

'Oh yes, his driver's licence. We never accept cheques without proper identification.'

'Can I see that?' Genero asked. Willis handed him the cheque. 'Carrier Avenue,' Genero said. 'Where's that?'

'Downtown,' Willis answered. 'In The Quarter.'

'What do you take in your tea, gentlemen?' Flora asked.

They sat sipping tea in the living-room streaming with sunlight. Once, during a lull in the small talk over their steaming cups, Genero asked, 'Why'd you name your store The Monkey Wrench?'

'Why not?' Frieda answered.

It was clearly time to go.

The curious thing about fishing in the sewer for those Hallowe'en masks was that it filled Brown with a sense of exhilaration he had not known since he was a boy. He could remember a hundred past occasions when he and his childhood friends had removed an iron sewer grating and climbed down into the muck to retrieve a rubber ball hit by a stickball bat, or an immie carelessly aimed, or even now and then a dime or a quarter that had slipped from a clenched fist and rolled down into the kerbside drain. He was too large now to squeeze through the narrow opening of the sewer, but he could see at least one of the masks some five feet below him, resting on the pipe elbow in a brownish paper-littered slime. He stretched out flat on the pavement, head twisted away from the kerb and tried to reach the mask. His arm, long as it was, was not long enough. His fingertips wiggled below, touching nothing but stagnant air. He got to his feet, brushed off the knees of his trousers and the elbows of his coat, and then looked up the block. Not a kid in sight. Never a kid around when you needed one. He began searching his pockets. He found a paper clip holding a business card to one of the pages in his pad. He removed the clip, put the card into his wallet, and then took a sheaf of evidence tags from his inside jacket pocket. Each of the tags had a short length of string tied through a hole at one end. He unfastened the strings from ten tags, knotted them all together and came up with a five-foot-long piece of string. He opened the paper clip so that it resembled a fish hook, and then tied it to one end of the string. Weighting the line with a duplicate key to his station house locker, he grinned and began fishing in the sewer. On the twentieth try, he hooked the narrow piece of elastic clipped to the mask. Slowly, carefully, patiently, he reeled in his line.

He was looking at a somewhat soiled Snow White, but this was the seventies, and nobody expected to find virgins in sewers any more.

Still grinning, Brown replaced the grating, brushed himself off again, and headed back for the squad-room.

In the city for which Brown worked, the Identification Section and the Police Laboratory operated on weekends with only a skeleton force, which was often only slightly better than operating with no force at all. Most cases got put over till Monday, unless they were terribly urgent. The shooting of a police detective was considered terribly urgent, and so the Snow White mask Brown dispatched to the lab downtown on High Street was given top priority. Detective-Lieutenant Sam Grossman, who ran the lab, was of course not working on a Sunday. The task of examining the mask for latent fingerprints (or indeed *any* clue as to its wearer's identity) fell to Detective/3rd Grade Marshall Davies, who, like Genero, was a comparatively new detective and therefore prone to catching weekend duty at the lab. He promised Brown he would get back to him as soon as possible, mindful of the fact that a detective had been shot and that there might be all kinds of pressure from upstairs, and then set to work.

In the squad-room, Brown replaced the telephone on its cradle and looked up as a patrolman approached the slatted rail divider with a prisoner in tow. At his desk, Carl Kapek was eating an early lunch, preparatory to heading for the bar in which the marine had encountered the girl with the bewitching behind, bars in this city being closed on Sundays until twelve, at which time it was presumably acceptable for churchgoers to begin getting drunk. The clock on the squad-room wall read fifteen minutes to noon. The squad-room was somewhat more crowded than it might have been at this hour on a Sunday because Levine, Di Maeo and Meriwether, the three detectives who had been called in when they were supposed to be on vacation, were sitting at one of the desks waiting to see the lieutenant, who at the moment was talking to Captain Frick, commander of the precinct, about the grocery store shooting and the necessity to get some more men on it. The three detectives were naturally grumbling. Di Maeo said that next time he was going to Puerto Rico on his vacation because then the lieutenant could shove it up his ass if he wanted him to come back. Cooperman was on vacation, too, wasn't he? But he was in the Virgin Islands, and the loot sure as hell didn't call *him* down there and drag *him* in, did he? Besides, Levine pointed out, Andy Parker was a lousy cop and who the hell cared if he got shot or even killed? Meriwether, who was a mild-mannered hair-bag in his early sixties, and a detective/first to boot, said, 'Now, now, fellows, it's all part of the game, all part of the game,' and Di Maeo belched.

The patrolman walked over to Brown's desk, told his prisoner to sit down, took Brown aside, and whispered something to him. Brown nodded and came back to the desk. The prisoner was handcuffed, sitting with his hands in his lap. He was a pudgy little man with green eyes and a pencil-line moustache. Brown estimated his age at forty or thereabouts. He was wearing a brown overcoat, a brown suit and shoes, white shirt with a button-down collar, gold-and-brown striped silk tie. Brown asked the patrolman to advise the man of his rights, a job the patrolman accepted with some trepidation, while he called the hospital to ask about Parker's condition. They told him that Parker was doing fine. Brown accepted the report without noticeable enthusiasm. He hung up the phone, heard the prisoner tell the patrolman he had nothing to hide and would answer any questions they wanted to ask, swivelled his chair around to face the man, and said, 'What's your name?'

The man would not look Brown in the eye. Instead, he kept staring past his left ear to the grilled windows and the sky outside.

'Perry Lyons,' he said. His voice was very low. Brown could barely hear him.

'What were you doing in the park just now, Lyons?' Brown said.

'Nothing,' Lyons answered.

'Speak up!' Brown snapped. There was a noticeable edge to his voice. The patrolman, too, was staring down at Lyons in what could only be described as an extremely hostile way, his brow twisted into a frown, his eyes hard and mean, his lips tightly compressed, his arms folded across his chest.

'I wasn't doing nothing,' Lyons answered.

'Patrolman Brogan here seems to think otherwise.'

Lyons shrugged.

'What about it, Lyons?'

'There's no law against talking to somebody.'

'Who were you talking to, Lyons?'

'A kid.'

'What'd you say to him?'

'Just it was a nice day, that's all.'

'That's not what the kid told Patrolman Brogan.'

'Well, kids, you know kids,' Lyons said.

'How old was the kid, Joe?' Brown asked.

'About nine,' Brogan answered.

'You always talk to nine-year-old kids in the park?' Brown asked.

'Sometimes.'

'How often?'

'There's no law against talking to kids. I like kids.'

'I'll bet you do,' Brown said. 'Tell him what the boy told you, Brogan.'

Brogan hesitated a moment, and then said, 'The boy said you asked him to blow you, Lyons.'

'No,' Lyons said. 'No, I never said anything like that. You're mistaken.'

'I'm not mistaken,' Brogan said.

'Well then, the kid's mistaken. He never heard anything like that from me, nossir.'

'You ever been arrested before?' Brogan asked.

Lyons did not answer.

'Come on,' Brown said impatiently, 'we can check it in a minute.'

'Well, yes,' Lyons said. 'I have been arrested before.'

'How many times?'

'Twice.'

'What for?'

'Well . . .' Lyons said, and shrugged.

'What *for*, Lyons?'

'Well, it was, uh, I got in trouble with somebody a while back.'

'What kind of trouble?'

'With some kid.'

'What was the charge, Lyons?'

Lyons hesitated again.

'What was the charge?' Brown repeated.

'Carnal Abuse.'

'You're a child molester, huh, Lyons?'

'No, no, it was a bum rap.'

'Were you convicted?'

'Yes, but that don't mean a thing, you guys know that. The kid was lying. He wanted to get even with me, he wanted to get me in trouble, so he told all kinds of lies about me. Hell, what would I want to fool around with a kid like that for? I had a girlfriend and everything, this waitress, you know? A real pretty girl, what would I want to fool around with a little kid for?'

'You tell me.'

S–F

'It was a bum rap, that's all. These things happen, that's all. You guys know that.'

'And the second arrest?'

'Well, that . . .'

'Yeah?'

'Well, you see what happened, after I got parolled, you know, I went back to live in this motel I used to live in before I got put away, you know?'

'Where'd you serve your time?'

'Castleview.'

'Go ahead.'

'So I had this same room, you know? That I had before they locked me up. And it turned out the kid who got me in trouble before, he was living there with his mother.'

'Just by coincidence, huh?'

'Well, no, not by coincidence. I mean, I can't claim it was coincidence. His mother ran the place, you see. I mean, she and her father owned it together. So it wasn't coincidence, you know. But I didn't think the kid was going to cause me no more trouble, you see what I mean? I done my time, he already got even with me, so I didn't expect no more trouble from him. Only thing is he come around to my cabin one day, and he made me do things to him. He said he'd tell his mother I was bothering him again if I didn't do these things to him. I mean, I was on parole, you know what I mean? If the kid had went to his mother, they'd have packed me off again in a minute.'

'So what *did* you do, Lyons?'

'Argh, the fuckin' little bastard started yelling. They . . . they busted me again.'

'Same charge?'

'Well, not the same 'cause the kid was older now. You know, like there's Carnal Abuse with a kid ten years old or younger, and then there's Carnal Abuse with a kid over ten and less than sixteen. He was eight years old the first time and eleven the next time. It was a bum rap both times. Who the hell needs that kind of stuff, you think I need it? Anyway, this was a long time ago. I already served *both* sentences. You think I'd be crazy enough to risk a third fall?'

'You could've been put away for life the *second* time,' Brown said.

'Don't you think I know it? So why would I take another chance?' He looked up at Brogan. 'That kid must've heard me wrong, Officer. I didn't say nothing like that to him. Honest. I really didn't.'

'We're booking you for Endangering the Morals of a Child, as defined in Section 483-a of the Penal Law,' Brown said. 'You're allowed three telephone . . .'

'Hey, hey, look,' Lyons said, 'give me a break, will you? I didn't mean no harm to the kid. I swear it. We were just sitting there talking, I swear to God. I *never* said nothing like that to him, would I say something like that to a little kid? Jesus, what do you take me for? Hey, come on, give me a break, will you? Come on, Officer, give me a break.'

'I'd advise you to get a lawyer,' Brown said. 'You want to take him down, Brogan?'

'Hey, come on,' Lyons said.

Brown watched as the patrolman led Lyons out of the squad-room. He stared at the retreating figure, and thought *The guy's sick, why the hell are we sending him away again, instead of helping him,* and then he thought *I have a seven-year-old daughter* – and then he stopped thinking because everything seemed suddenly too complex, and the telephone on his desk was ringing.

He lifted the receiver.

It was Steve Carella reporting that he was on his way to the squad-room.

José Vicente Huerta was in a bad way. Both of his legs had been broken by the four assailants who'd attacked him, and his face was swathed in bandages that covered the multiple wounds that had spilled his blood all over the front stoop of the building. He resembled a not so invisible Invisible Man, his brown eyes burning fiercely through the holes left in the bandages.

His mouth, pink against the white, showed through

another hole below the eye holes, and looked like a gaping
wound itself. He was conscious now, but the doctors advised
Delgado that their patient was heavily sedated and might
drift in and out of sleep as he talked. Delgado figured he
would take his chances.

He sat in a chair by the side of Huerta's bed. Huerta, both
legs in traction, his hands lying on the covers, palms up, his
head turned into the pillow in Delgado's direction, the
brown eyes burning fiercely, the wound of the mouth open
and pathetically vulnerable, listened as Delgado identified
himself, and then nodded when asked if he felt able to
answer some questions.

'First,' Delgado said, 'do you know who the men were?'

'No,' Huerta answered.

'You didn't recognize any of them?'

'No.'

'Were they young men?'

'I don't know.'

'You saw them as they attacked you, didn't you?'

'Yes.'

'Well, how old would you say they were?'

'I don't know.'

'Were they neighbourhood men?'

'I don't know.'

'Mr Huerta, any information you can give us . . .'

'I don't know who they were,' Huerta said.

'They hurt you very badly. Surely . . .'

The bandaged head turned away from Delgado, into the
pillow.

'Mr Huerta?'

Huerta did not answer.

'Mr Huerta?'

Again, he did not answer. As had been promised by the
doctors, he seemed to have drifted off into sleep. Delgado
sighed and stood up. Since he was at Buenavista Hospital,
anyway, and just so his visit shouldn't be a total loss, he
decided to stop in on Andy Parker to see how he was doing.
Parker was doing about as well as Huerta. He, too, was

asleep. The intern on the floor informed Delgado that Parker was out of danger.

Delgado seemed as thrilled by the information as Brown had earlier been.

The trouble with being a detective in any given neighbourhood is that almost everybody in the neighbourhood knows you're a detective. Since detection is supposed to be undercover secret stuff at least some of the time, snooping around becomes a little difficult when 90 per cent of the people you encounter know you're a snoop. The bartender at Bar Seventeen (which was the name of the bar in which the marine had first encountered the girl who later kicked him in the head, such bar being thus imaginatively named since it was located on Seventeenth Street) knew that Carl Kapek was a bull, and Kapek knew that the bartender knew, and since they *both* knew, neither of them made any pretence of playing at cops and robbers. The bartender set up beers for Kapek, who was not supposed to drink on duty, and Kapek accepted them without offering payment, and everybody had a nice little understanding going. Kapek did not even attempt to ask the bartender about the kicking girl and her boyfriend. Nor did the bartender try to find out why Kapek was there. If he was there, he was there for a reason, and the bartender knew it, and Kapek knew he knew it, and so the two men kept a respectful distance, coming into contact only when the bartender refilled Kapek's glass from time to time. It was a cool symbiosis. The bartender merely hoped that Kapek was not there investigating some minor violation that would inevitably cost him money. He was already paying off two guys from the Fire Department, not to mention the police sergeant on the beat; one more guy with his hand out, and it would be cheaper to take care of the goddamn violations instead. Kapek, for his part, merely hoped that the bartender would not indicate to too many of his early afternoon patrons that the big blond guy sitting at the bar was a police detective. It was difficult enough these days to earn a living.

The way he decided to earn his living on this particular bright October Sunday – bright *outside*, dim and cheerless inside – was to engage a drunk in conversation. Kapek had been in the bar for close to an hour now, studying the patrons, trying to decide which of them were regulars, which of them came here infrequently, which of them recognized him from around the streets, which of them had not the faintest inkling that he was fuzz. He did all of this in what he hoped was a surreptitious manner, going to the phone booth once to pretend he was making a call, going to the men's room once, going to the jukebox three or four times, casing everyone in the place on his various excursions, and then settling down on a stool within listening distance of the bartender and a man in a dark blue suit. Kapek opened the Sunday tabloid he had carried with him into the bar, and turned to the sports section. He pretended to be pondering yesterday's racing results, working figures with a pencil in the margin of the newspaper, while simultaneously listening intently to everything the man in the blue suit said. When the bartender walked off to serve someone at the other end of the bar, Kapek made his move.

'Damn horse never delivers when he's supposed to,' he said.

'I beg your pardon?' the man in the blue suit said, turning on his stool. He was already very intoxicated, having presumably begun his serious drinking at home before the bar could legally open its doors. He looked at Kapek now with the benign expression of someone anxious to be friendly with anyone at all, even if he happened to be a cop. He did not seem to know that Kapek was a cop, nor was Kapek anxious to let him in on the secret.

'You follow the ponies?' Kapek asked.

'I permit myself a tiny wager every so often,' the man in the blue suit said. He had bleary blue eyes and a veined nose. His white shirt looked unironed, his solid blue tie was haphazardly knotted, his suit rumpled. He kept his right hand firmly clutched around a water tumbler full of whisky on the bar top in front of him.

'This nag's the goddamn favourite nine times out of ten,'

Kapek said, 'but he never wins when he's supposed to. I think the jocks got it all fixed between them.'

The bartender was ambling back. Kapek shot him a warning glance: *Stay out of this, pal. You work your side of the street, I'll work mine.* The bartender hesitated in mid-stride then turned on his heel and walked over to his other customer.

'My name's Carl Kapek,' Kapek said, and closed his newspaper, encouraging further conversation. 'I've been playing the horses for twelve years now, I made only one decent killing in all that time.'

'How much?' the man in the blue suit asked.

'Four hundred dollars on a long shot. Had two dollars on his nose. It was beautiful, beautiful,' Kapek said, and grinned and shook his head remembering the beauty of this event that had never taken place. The most he had ever won in his life was a chemistry set at a church bazaar.

'How long ago was that?' the man in the blue suit asked.

'Six years ago,' Kapek said, and laughed.

'That's a long time between drinks,' the man said, and laughed with him.

'I don't think I got your name,' Kapek said, and extended his hand.

'Leonard Sutherland,' the man said. 'My friends all call me Lennie.'

'How do you do, Lennie?' Kapek said, and they shook hands.

'What do *your* friends all call *you*?' Lennie asked.

'Carl.'

'Nice meeting you, Carl,' Lennie said.

'A pleasure,' Kapek answered.

'*My* game's poker,' Lennie said. Playing the horses, you'll pardon me, is for suckers. Poker's a game of skill.'

'No question,' Kapek agreed.

'Do you actually *prefer* beer?' Lennie asked suddenly.

'What?'

'I notice you have been drinking beer exclusively. If you would permit me, Carl, I'd consider it an honour to buy you something stronger.'

'Little early in the day for me,' Kapek said, and smiled apologetically.

'Never too early for a little rammer,' Lennie said, and smiled.

'Well, I was out drinking late last night,' Kapek said, and shrugged.

'I am out drinking late *every* night,' Lennie said, 'but it's still never too early for a little rammer.' To emphasize his theory, he lifted the water glass and swallowed half the whisky in it. 'Mmm, boy,' he said, and coughed.

'You usually do your drinking here?' Kapek asked.

'Hm?' Lennie asked. His eyes were watering. He took a handkerchief from his back pocket and dabbed at them. He coughed again.

'In this place?'

'Oh, I drift around, drift around,' Lennie said, and made a fluttering little motion with the fingers of one hand.

'Reason I ask,' Kapek said, 'is I was in here last night, and I didn't happen to see you.'

'Oh, I was here all right,' Lennie said, which Kapek already knew because this was what he had overheard in the conversation between Lennie and the bartender, a passing reference to a minor event that had taken place in Bar Seventeen the night before, the bartender having had to throw out a twenty-year-old who was noisily expressing his views on lowering the age to vote.

'Were you here when they threw out that young kid?' Kapek asked.

'Oh, indeed,' Lennie said.

'Didn't see you,' Kapek said.

'Oh yes, here indeed,' Lennie said.

'There was a marine . . .' Kapek said tentatively.

'Hm?' Lennie asked with a polite smile, and then lifted his glass and threw down the rest of the whisky. He said, 'Mmm, boy,' coughed again, dabbed at his watering eyes, and then said, 'Yes, yes, but he came in later.'

'After they threw that kid out, you mean?'

'Oh yes, much later. Were you here when the marine came in?'

'Oh, sure,' Kapek said.

'Funny we didn't notice each other,' Lennie said, and shrugged and signalled to the bartender. The bartender slouched towards them, shooting Kapek his own warning glance: *This guy's a good steady customer. If I lose him 'cause you're pumping him for information here, I'm gonna get sore as hell.*

'Yeah, Lennie?' the bartender said.

'I'll have another double, please,' Lennie answered. 'And please see what my friend here is having, won't you?'

The bartender shot the warning glance at Kapek again. Kapek stared back at him implacably and said, 'I'll just have another beer.' The bartender nodded and walked off.

'There was this girl in here about then,' Kapek said to Lennie. 'You remember her?'

'Which girl?'

'Coloured girl in a red dress,' Kapek said.

Lennie was watching the bartender as he poured whisky into the tumbler. 'Hm?' he said.

'Coloured girl in a red dress,' Kapek repeated.

'Oh yes, Belinda,' Lennie answered.

'Belinda what?'

'Don't know,' Lennie said.

His eyes brightened as the bartender came back with his whisky and Kapek's beer. Lennie lifted the tumbler immediately and drank. 'Mmm, boy,' he said, and coughed. The bartender hovered near them. Kapek met his eyes, decided if he wanted so badly to get in on the act, he'd let him.

'Would *you* happen to know?' Kapek said.

'Know what?'

'There was a girl named Belinda in here last night. Wearing a red dress. Would you know her last name?'

'Me,' the bartender said, 'I'm deaf, dumb, and blind.' He paused. 'This guy's a cop, Lennie, did you know that?'

'Oh yes, certainly,' Lennie said, and fell off his stool and passed out cold.

Kapek got up, bent, seized Lennie under the arms and dragged him over to one of the booths. He loosened his tie and then looked up at the bartender, who had come over and was standing with his hands on his hips.

'You always serve booze to guys who've had too much?' he asked.

'You always ask them questions?' the bartender said.

'Let's ask *you* a couple instead, okay?' Kapek said. 'Who's Belinda?'

'Never heard of her.'

'Okay. Just make sure *she* never hears of *me*.'

'Huh?'

'You were pretty anxious just now to let our friend here know I was a cop. I'm telling you something straight, pal. I'm looking for Belinda, who*ever* the hell she is. If she finds out about it, from whatever source, I'm going to assume you're the one who tipped her. And that might just make you an accessory, pal.'

'Who you trying to snow?' the bartender said. 'I run a clean joint here. I don't know nobody named Belinda, and whatever she doné or didn't do, I'm out of it completely. So what's this "accessory" crap?'

'Try to forget I was in here looking for her,' Kapek said. 'Otherwise you're liable to find out *just* what this "accessory" crap is. Okay?'

'You scare me to death,' the bartender said.

'You know where Lennie lives?' Kapek asked.

'Yeah.'

'He married?'

'Yeah.'

'Call his wife. Tell her to come down here and get him.'

'She'll kill him,' the bartender said. He looked down at Lennie and shook his head. 'I'll sober him up and get him home, don't worry about it.'

He was already talking gently and kindly to the unconscious Lennie as Kapek went out of the bar.

*   *   *

Ramon Castañeda was in his undershirt when he opened the door for Delgado.

'*Sí, qué quiere usted?*' he asked.

'I'm Detective Delgado, Eighty-seventh Squad,' Delgado said, and flipped his wallet open to show his shield. Castañeda looked at it closely.

'What's the trouble?' he asked.

'May I come in, please?' Delgado said.

'Who is it, Ray?' a woman called from somewhere in the apartment.

'Policeman,' Castañeda said over his shoulder. 'Come in,' he said to Delgado.

Delgado went into the apartment. There was a kitchen on his right, a living-room dead ahead, two bedrooms beyond that. The woman who came out of the closest bedroom was wearing a brightly flowered nylon robe and carrying a hair-brush in her right hand. She was quite beautiful, with long black hair and a pale complexion, grey-green eyes, a full bosom, ripely curving hips. She was barefoot, and she moved soundlessly into the living-room, and stood with her legs slightly apart, the hairbrush held just above her hip, somewhat like a hatchet she had just unsheathed.

'Sorry to bother you this way,' Delgado said.

'What is it?' the woman said.

'This is my wife,' Castañeda said. 'Rita, this is Detective ... what's your name again?'

'Delgado.'

'You Spanish?'

'Yes.'

'Good,' Castañeda said.

'What is it?' Rita said again.

'Your partner José Huerta ...'

'What's the matter with him?' Castañeda asked immediately. 'Is something the matter with him?'

'Yes. He was attacked by four men this morning ...'

'Oh, my God!' Rita said, and brought the hand holding the hairbrush to her mouth, pressing the back of it to her lips as though stifling a scream.

'Who?' Castañeda said. 'Who did it?'

'We don't know. He's at Buenavista Hospital now.' Delgado paused. 'Both his legs were broken.'

'Oh, my God!' Rita said again.

'We'll go to him at once,' Castañeda said, and turned away, ready to leave the room, seemingly anxious to dress and leave for the hospital immediately.

'If I may ...' Delgado said, and Castañeda remembered he was there, and paused, still on the verge of departure, and impatiently said to his wife, 'Get dressed, Rita,' and then said to Delgado, 'Yes, what is it? We want to see Joe as soon as possible.'

'I'd like to ask some questions before you go,' Delgado said.

'Yes, certainly.'

'How long have you and Mr Huerta been partners?'

The woman had not left the room. She stood standing slightly apart from the two men, the hairbrush bristles cradled on the palm of one hand, the other hand clutched tightly around the handle, her eyes wide as she listened.

'I told you to get dressed,' Castañeda said to her.

She seemed about to answer him. Then she gave a brief complying nod, wheeled, and went into the bedroom, closing the door only partially behind her.

'We have been partners for two years,' Castañeda said.

'Get along with each other?'

'Of course. Why?' Castañeda put his hands on his hips. He was a small man, perhaps five feet seven inches tall, and not particularly good-looking, with a pockmarked face and a longish nose and a moustache that sat just beneath it and somehow emphasized its length. He leaned towards Delgado belligerently now, defying him to explain that last question, his brown eyes burning as fiercely as had his partner's through the hospital bandages.

'A man has been assaulted, Mr Castañeda. It's routine to question his relatives and associates. I meant no ...'

'It sounded like you meant plenty,' Castañeda said. His hands were still on his hips. He looked like a fighting rooster

Delgado had once seen in a cock fight in the town of Vega
Baja, when he had gone back to the island to visit his dying
grandmother.

'Let's not get excited,' Delgado said. There was a note of
warning in his voice. The note informed Castañeda that
whereas both men were Puerto Ricans, one of them was a
cop entitled to ask questions about a third Puerto Rican who
had been badly beaten up. The note further informed
Castañeda that however mild Delgado's manner might
appear, he wasn't about to take any crap, and Castañeda
had better understand that right from go. Castañeda took
his hands from his hips. Delgado stared at him a moment
longer.

'Would you happen to know whether or not your partner
had any enemies?' he asked. His voice was flat. Through the
partially open door of the bedroom, he saw Rita Castañeda
move towards the dresser, and then away from it, out of
sight.

'No enemies that I know of,' Castañeda replied.

'Would you know if he'd ever received any threatening
letters or phone calls?'

'Never.'

The flowered robe flashed into view again. Delgado's eyes
flicked momentarily towards the open door. Castañeda
frowned.

'Would you have had any business deals recently that
caused any hard feelings with anyone?'

'None,' Castañeda said. He moved towards the open bedroom door, took the knob in his hand, and pulled the door
firmly shut. 'We're real estate agents for apartment buildings. We rent apartments. It's as simple as that.'

'No trouble with any of the tenants?'

'We hardly ever come into contact with them. Once in a
while we have trouble collecting the rents. But that's normal
in this business, and nobody bears a grudge.'

'Would you say your partner is well liked?'

Castañeda shrugged.

'What does that mean, Mr Castañeda?'

'Well liked, who knows? He's a man like any other man. He is liked by some and disliked by others.'

'Who *dislikes* him?' Delgado asked immediately.

'No one dislikes him enough to have him beaten up,' Castañeda said.

'I see,' Delgado answered. He smiled pleasantly. 'Well,' he said, 'thank you for your information. I won't keep you any longer.'

'Fine, fine,' Castañeda said. He went to the front door and opened it. 'Let me know if you find the men who did it,' he said.

'I will,' Delgado answered, and found himself in the hallway. The door closed behind him. In the apartment, he heard Castañeda shout, 'Rita *esta lista?*'

He put his ear to the door.

He could hear Castañeda and his wife talking very quietly inside the apartment, their voices rumbling distantly, but he could not tell what they were saying. Only once, when Rita raised her voice, did Delgado catch a word.

The word was *hermano*, which in Spanish meant 'brother'.

It was close to 2 PM, and things were pretty quiet in the squad-room.

Kapek was looking through the Known Muggers file, trying to get a lead on the black girl known only as Belinda. Carella had arrived in time to have lunch with Brown, and both men sat at a long table near one of the windows, one end of it burdened with fingerprinting equipment, eating tuna fish sandwiches and drinking coffee in cardboard containers. As they ate, Brown filled him in on what he had so far. Marshall Davies at the lab, true to his word, had gone to work on the Snow White mask the moment he received it, and had reported back not a half-hour later. He had been able to recover only one good print, that being a thumbprint on the inside surface, presumably left there when the wearer was adjusting the mask to his face. He had sent this immediately to the Identification Section, where the men on Sunday duty had searched their Single fingerprint file, tracking

through a maze of arches, loops, whorls, scars, and acciden-
tals to come up with a positive identification for a man
named Bernard Goldenthal.

His yellow sheet was now on Brown's desk, and both detectives studied it carefully:

PRISONER'S CRIMINAL RECORD	POLICE DEPARTMENT	IDENTIFICATION SECTION

NAME __BERNARD GOLDENTHAL__   B. # 47-61042

ALIAS __"Bernie Gold," "Goldie," "Goldfinger."__   Y.S. # G-21-3479

DATE OF BIRTH __February 12, 1931__   F.B.I. # 74-01-22
                                                                    89234
FINGERPRINT CLASSIFICATION ___27 L 1 T r 20___
                                        L 1 U

This certifies that the finger impressions of the above-named person have
been compared and the following is a true copy of the records of this section.

Date of Arrest	Location	Charge	Arresting Officer	Date, Disposition, Judge and Court
5-7-47	Isola	Burg. Juv. Del.	D of C	Jewish Home for Boys
2-9-48	Calm's Point	Burg. Fin. Chg. Unlaw Entry	Wexner 75 Pct.	Judge McCarthy County Court
6-5-49	Isola	Robbery	Janus 19 Sqd.	6-30-49 Dismissed Judge Evans Sup. Court
8-17-49	Isola	Robbery Gun	Cowper 19 Sqd.	11-28-49 Discharged Judge Nastro Gen. Sess.
1-21-51	Riverhead	Gr. Laro 1st Burg. 3rd	Franklin	3-11-51 5 to 10 Yrs. on Gr. Laro. 5 to 10 Yrs. on Burg. 3rd. Judge Lefkin, County Court.
12-19-59	Isola	Theft from Interstate Shipment	F.B.I.	3 yrs to serve followed by 10 yrs probation Judge O'Hare U.S. So. Dist. Court.
12-23-69	Isola	974 PL	Magruder 2 Div	1-28-70 $50.or 10 days Judge Fields Spec. Sess.
2-9-70	Isola	974 PL	Donovan 2 Div	1-28-70 $100/30 days Judge Fields Spec. Sess.
9-19-70	Isola	974a PL	Donato CIU	11-25-70 Gen.Sess. Unl. Poss. Policy Slips $150 or 60 days. Ashworth.

A man's yellow sheet (so called because the record actually
was duplicated on a yellow sheet of paper; bar owners were
not the *only* imaginative people in this city) was perhaps not
as entertaining, say, as a good novel, but it did have a short-
hand narrative power all its own. Goldenthal's record had
the added interest of a rising dramatic line, a climax of sorts,
and then a slackening of tension just before the denouement
– which was presumably yet to come.

His first arrest had been at the age of sixteen, for Burglary
and Juvenile Delinquency, and he had been remanded to
the Jewish Home for Boys, a correctional institution. Less
than a year later, apparently back on the streets again, he
had been arrested again for Burglary, with the charge reduced to Unlawful Entry and (the record was incomplete
here) the courts had apparently shown leniency in con-
sideration of his age – he was barely seventeen at the time –
and let him off scot-free. Progressing to bigger and better
things during the next year, he was arrested first on a Robbery charge and then on a Robbery with a Gun charge, and
again the courts showed mercy and let him go. Thus em-
boldened and encouraged, he moved on to Grand Larceny
First and Burglary Third, was again busted and this time
was sent to prison. He had probably served both terms con-
currently, and was released on parole sometime before 1959,
when apparently he decided to knock over a truck crossing
state lines, thereby inviting the Federal Bureau of Investigation to step in. Carella and Brown figured the '3 yrs to
serve' were the three years remaining from his prior conviction; the courts were again being lenient.

And perhaps this leniency was finally paying off. The violations he'd been convicted of since his second release from
prison were not too terribly serious, especially when compared to Grand Larceny or Interstate Theft. Section 974 of
the Penal Law was defined as 'keeping a place for or trans-
ferring money in the game of policy', and was a misdemeanour. Section 974a was a bit heavier – 'Operating a
policy business' – and was a felony punishable by impris-
onment for a term not exceeding five years. In either case,

Goldenthal seemed to have moved into a more respectable line of work, employing himself in the 'policy' or 'numbers game', which many hard-working citizens felt was a perfectly harmless recreation and hardly anything for the Law to get all excited about. The Law had not, in fact, got too terribly excited about Goldenthal's most recent offences. He could have got five years on his last little adventure, when in fact all he had drawn was a fine of a hundred and fifty dollars or sixty days, on a reduced charge of Unlawful Possession of Policy Slips, Section 975 of the Penal Law.

Goldenthal had begun his criminal career at the age of sixteen. He was now almost forty years old, and had spent something better than ten years of his adult life in prison. If they found him, and busted him again, and convicted him of the grocery store holdup and murder, he would be sent away for ever.

There were several other pieces of information in the packet the IS had sent uptown – a copy of Goldenthal's fingerprint card, with a complete description of him on the reverse side; a final report from his probation officer back in '69; a copy of the Detective Division report on his most recent arrest – but the item of chief interest to Carella and Brown was Goldenthal's last known address. He had apparently been living in uptown Isola with his mother, a Mrs Minnie Goldenthal, until the time of her death three months ago. He had then moved to an apartment downtown, and was presumably still living there.

They decided to hit it together.

They were no fools.

Goldenthal had once been arrested on a gun charge, and either he or his partner had put three bullets into two men not seven hours before.

The show began ten minutes after Carella and Brown left the squad-room. It had a cast of four and was titled *Hookers' Parade*. It starred two young streetwalkers who billed themselves as Rebecca and Sally Good.

'Those are not your real names,' Kapek insisted.

'Those are our real names,' Sally answered, 'and you can all go to hell.'

The other two performers in the show were the patrolman who had answered the complaint and made the arrest, and a portly gentleman in a pin-striped suit who looked mortally offended though not at all embarrassed, rather like a person who had wet his pyjamas in a hospital bed, where illness is expected and annoying but certainly nothing to be ashamed of.

'All right, what's the story, Phil?' Kapek asked the patrolman.

'Well, what happened . . .'

'If you don't mind,' the portly gentleman said, 'I am the injured party here.'

'Who the hell injured you, would you mind telling me?' Rebecca said.

'All right, let's calm down here,' Kapek said. He had finished with the Known Muggers file and was anxious to get to the Modus Operandi file, and he found all this tumult distracting. The girls, one black and one white, were both wearing tan sweaters, suède miniskirts, and brown boots. Sally, the white one, had long blonde hair. Rebecca, the black one, had her hair done in an Afro cut and bleached blonde. They were both in their early twenties, both quite attractive, long and leggy and busty and brazen and cheap as a bottle of ninety-cent wine. The portly gentleman sat some distance away from them, on the opposite side of Kapek's desk, as though afraid of contracting some dreaded disease. His face was screwed into an offended frown, his eyes sparkled with indignation.

'I wish these young ladies arrested,' he said. 'I am the man who made the complaint, the injured party, and I am willing to press charges, and I wish them arrested at once.'

'Fine, Mr . . .' Kapek consulted his pad. 'Mr Searle,' he said. 'Do you want to tell me what happened?'

'I am from Independence, Missouri,' Searle said. 'The home of Harry S. Truman.'

'Yes, sir,' Kapek said.

'Big deal,' Sally said.

'I'm here in the city on business,' Searle said. 'I usually stay midtown, but I have several appointments in this area tomorrow morning, and I thought it would be more convenient to find lodgings in the neighbourhood.' He paused and cleared his throat. 'There is a rather nice hotel overlooking the park. The Grover.'

'Yes, sir,' Kapek said.

'Or at least *I thought* it was a rather nice hotel.'

'It's a fleabag,' Rebecca said.

'How about knocking it off?' Kapek said.

'What the hell for? This hick blows the whistle for no reason at all, and we're supposed . . .'

'Let's hear what the man has to say, okay?' Kapek said sharply.

'Okay,' Rebecca said.

'*Whatever* he has to say,' Sally said, 'he's full of crap.'

'Listen, sister,' Kapek warned.

'Okay, okay,' Sally said, and tossed her long blonde hair. Rebecca crossed her legs, and lighted a cigarette. She blew the stream of smoke in Searle's direction, and he waved it away with his hands.

'Mr Searle?' Kapek prompted.

'I was sitting in my room reading the *Times*,' Searle said, 'when a knock sounded on the door.'

'When was this, Mr Searle?'

'An hour ago? I'm not sure.'

'What time did you catch the squeal, Phil?'

'One-twenty.'

'Just *about* an hour ago,' Kapek said.

'Then it must have been a little earlier than that,' Searle said. 'They must have arrived at about one-ten or thereabouts.'

'Who's that, Mr Searle?'

'These young ladies,' he answered, without looking at them.

'They knocked on your door?'

'They did.'

'And then what?'

'I opened the door. They were standing there in the corridor. Both of them. They said . . .' Searle shook his head. 'This is entirely inconceivable to me.'

'What did they say?'

'They said the elevator operator told them I wanted some action, and they were there to supply it. I didn't know what they meant at first. I asked them what they meant. They told me exactly what they meant.'

'What did they tell you, Mr Searle?'

'Do we have to go into this?'

'If you're going to press charges, why, yes, I guess we do. I'm not sure yet what these girls did or said to . . .'

'They offered to sleep with me,' Searle said, and looked away.

'Who the hell would want to sleep with *you*?' Sally muttered.

'Got to be out of your mind,' Rebecca said, and blew another stream of smoke at him.

'They told me they would *both* like to sleep with me,' Searle said. 'Together.'

'Uh-huh,' Kapek said, and glanced at Rebecca. 'Is that right?' he asked.

'Nope,' Rebecca answered.

'So, okay, what happened next?' Kapek said.

'I told them to come back in five minutes.'

'Why'd you tell them that?'

'Because I wanted to inform the police.'

'And did you?'

'I did.'

'And did the girls come back?'

'In seven minutes. I clocked them.'

'And then what?'

'They came into the room and said it would be fifty dollars for each of them. I told them that was very expensive. They both took off their sweaters to show me what I would be getting for the money. Neither of them was wearing a brassiere.'

'Is that right?' Kapek asked.

'Nobody wears bras today,' Sally said.

'Nobody,' Rebecca said.

'That don't make us hookers,' Sally said.

'Ask the officer here in what condition he found them when he entered the room.'

'Phil?'

'Naked from the waist up,' the patrolman said.

'I wish them arrested,' Searle said. 'For prostitution.'

'You got some case, Fatty,' Rebecca said.

'You know what privates are, Fatty,' Sally asked.

'Must I be submitted to this kind of talk?' Searle said. 'Surely . . .'

'Knock it off,' Kapek said to the girls. 'What they're trying to tell you, Mr Searle, is that it's extremely difficult in this city to make a charge of prostitution stick unless the woman has exposed her privates, do you see what I mean? Her genitals,' Kapek said. 'That's been our experience. That's what it is,' he concluded, and shrugged. Rebecca and Sally were smiling.

'They did expose themselves to me,' Searle said.

'Yes, but not the privates, you see. They have to expose the privates. That's the yardstick, you see. For arrest. To make a conviction stick. That's been the, you see, experience of the police department in such matters. Now, of course, we can always book them for disorderly conduct . . .'

'Yes, do that,' Searle said.

'That's Section 722,' Kapek said, 'Subdivision 9, but then you'd have to testify in court that the girls were soliciting, you know, were hanging around a public place for the purpose of committing a crime against nature or any other lewdness. That's the way it's worded, that subdivision. So you'd have to explain in court what happened. I mean, what they said to you and all. You know what I mean, Mr Searle?'

'I think so, yes.'

'We could also get them on Section 887, Subdivision 4 of the Code of Criminal Procedure. That's, you know, inducing,

enticing or procuring another to commit lewdness, for-
nication...'

'Yes, yes, I quite understand,' Searle said, and waved his
hand as though clearing away smoke, though Rebecca had
not blown any in his direction.

'... unlawful sexual intercourse or any other indecent act,'
Kapek concluded. 'But there, too, you'd have to testify in
court.'

'Wouldn't the patrolman's word be enough? He saw them
all exposed that way.'

'Well, we got half a dozen plays running in this town
where the girls are naked from the waist up, and also down,
and that doesn't mean they're offering to commit prostitution.' Kapek turned to the patrolman. 'Phil, you hear them
say anything about prostitution?'

'Nope,' the patrolman answered, and grinned. He was obviously enjoying himself.

'*I* heard them,' Searle said.

'Sure. And like I said, if you're willing to testify in
court...'

'They're *obvious* prostitutes,' Searle said.

'Probably got records, too, no question,' Kapek said.
'But...'

'I've never been busted,' Sally said.

'How about you, Rebecca?' Kapek asked.

'If you're going to start asking me questions, I want a
lawyer. *That's* how about me.'

'Well, what do you say, Mr Searle? You want to go ahead
with this, or not?' Kapek asked.

'When would I have to go to court?'

'Prostitution cases usually get immediate hearings.
Dozens of them each day. I guess it would be tomorrow
sometime.'

'I have business to take care of tomorrow. That's why I'm
here to begin with.'

'Well,' Kapek said, and shrugged.

'I hate to let them get away with this,' Searle said.

'Why?' Sally asked. 'Who did you any harm?'

'You offended me gravely, young lady.'

'How?' Rebecca asked.

'Would you ask them to go, please?' Searle said.

'You've decided not to press charges?'

'That is my decision.'

'Beat it,' Kapek said to the girls. 'Keep your asses out of that hotel. Next time, you may not be so lucky.'

Neither of the girls said a word. Sally waited while Rebecca ground out her cigarette in the ashtray. Then they both swivelled out of the squad-room. Searle looked somewhat dazed. He sat staring ahead of him. Then he shook his head and said, 'When they think *that*, when they think a man needs *two* women, they're really thinking he can't even handle *one*.' He shook his head again, rose, put his homburg onto his head, and walked out of the squad-room. The patrolman tilted his nightstick at Kapek, and ambled out after him.

Kapek sighed and went to the Modus Operandi file.

The last known address for Bernard Goldenthal was on the North Side, all the way downtown in a warehouse district adjacent to the River Harb. The tenement in which he reportedly lived was shouldered between two huge edifices that threatened to squash it flat. The street was deserted. This was Sunday, and there was no traffic. Even the tugboats on the river, not two blocks away, seemed motionless. Carella and Brown went into the building, checked the mailboxes – there was a name in only one of them, and it was not Goldenthal's – and then went up to the third floor, where Goldenthal was supposed to be living in Apartment 3A. They listened outside the door, and heard nothing. Carella nodded to Brown, and Brown knocked.

'Who is it?' a man's voice asked from behind the door.

'Mr Goldenthal?' Brown asked.

'No,' the man answered. 'Who is it?'

Brown looked at Carella. Carella nodded.

'Police officers,' Brown said. 'Want to open up, please?'

There was a slight hesitation from behind the door. Carella unbuttoned his coat and put his hand on the butt of his revolver. The door opened. The man standing there was in his forties, perhaps as tall as Carella, heavier, with black hair that sprang from his scalp like weeds in a small garden, brown eyes opened wide in inquiry, thick black brows arched over them. Whoever he was, he did not by any stretch of the imagination fit the description on Goldenthal's fingerprint card.

'Yes?' he said. 'What is it?'

'We're looking for Bernard Goldenthal,' Brown said. 'Does he live here?'

'No, I'm sorry,' the man said. 'He doesn't.' He spoke quite softly, the way a very big man will sometimes speak to a child or an old person, as though compensating for his hugeness by lowering the volume of his voice.

'Our information says he lives here,' Carella said.

'Well, I'm sorry,' the man said, 'but he doesn't. He may have at one time, but he doesn't now.'

'What's *your* name?' Carella asked. His coat was still open, and his hand was resting lightly on his hip, close to his holster.

'Herbert Gross.'

'Mind if we come in, Mr Gross?'

'Why would you want to?' Gross asked.

'To see if Mr Goldenthal is here.'

'I just told you he wasn't,' Gross said.

'Mind if we check it for ourselves?' Brown said.

'I really don't see why I should let you,' Gross said.

'Goldenthal's a known criminal,' Carella said, 'and we're looking for him in connexion with a recent crime. The last address we have for him is 911 Forrester, Apartment 3A. This is 911 Forrester, Apartment 3A, and we'd like to come in and check on whether or not our information is correct.'

'Your information is wrong,' Gross insisted. 'It must be very old information.'

'No, it's recent information.'

'How recent?'

'Less than three months old.'

'Well, I've been living here for two months now, so he must have moved before that.'

'Are you going to let us in, Mr Gross?'

'No, I don't think so,' Gross said.

'Why not?'

'I don't think I like the idea of policemen crashing in here on a Sunday afternoon, that's all.'

'Anybody in there with you?'

'I don't think that's any of your business,' Gross said.

'Look, Mr Gross,' Brown said, 'we can come back here with a warrant, if that's what you'd like. Why not make it easy for us?'

'Why should I?'

'Why shouldn't you?' Carella said. 'Have you got anything to hide?'

'Nothing at all.'

'Then how about it?'

'Sorry,' Gross said, and closed the door and locked it.

The two detectives stood in the hallway and silently weighed their next move. There were two possibilities open to them, and both of them presented considerable risks. The first possibility was that Goldenthal was indeed in the apartment and armed, in which event he was now warned and if they kicked in the door he would open fire immediately. The second possibility was that the IS information *was* dated, and that Goldenthal had indeed moved from the apartment more than two months ago, in which event Gross would have a dandy case against the city if they kicked in the door and conducted an illegal search. Brown gestured with his head, and both men moved towards the stairwell, away from the door.

'What do you think?' Brown whispered.

'There were two of them on the grocery store job,' Carella said. 'Gross might just be the other man.'

'He fits the description I got from the old lady,' Brown said. 'Shall we kick it in?'

'I'd rather wait downstairs. He expects us to come back. If he's in this with Goldenthal, he's going to run, sure as hell.'

'Right,' Brown said. 'Let's split.'

They had parked Brown's sedan just outside the building. Knowing that Gross' apartment overlooked the street, and hoping that he was now watching them from his window, they got into the car and drove north towards the river. Brown turned right under the River Highway, and headed uptown. He turned right again at the next corner, and then drove back to Scovil Avenue and Forrester Street, where he pulled the car to the kerb. Both men got out.

'Think he's still watching?' Brown asked.

'I doubt it, but why take chances?' Carella said. 'The street's deserted. If we plant ourselves in one of the doorways on this end of the block, we can see anybody going in or out of his building.'

The first doorway they found had obviously been used as a nest by any number of vagrants. Empty pint bottles of whisky in brown paper bags littered the floor, together with empty crumpled cigarette packages, and empty half-gallon wine bottles, and empty candy bar wrappers. The stench of urine was overpowering.

'No job's worth *this*,' Brown said.

'Don't care if he killed the goddamn *governor*,' Carella said.

They walked swiftly into the clean brisk October air. Brown looked up the street towards Gross' building. Together, he and Carella ducked into the next doorway. It was better, but only a trifle so.

'Let's hope he makes his move fast,' Brown said.

'Let's hope so,' Carella agreed.

They did not have long to wait.

In five minutes flat, Gross came down the front steps of his building and began walking south, towards the building where they waited. They moved back against the wall. He walked past swiftly, without even glancing into the hallway. They gave him a good lead, and then took off after him, one on each side of the street, so that they formed an isosceles triangle with Gross at the point and Brown and Carella at either end of the base.

They lost him on Payne Avenue, when he boarded an uptown bus that left them running up behind it to choke in a cloud of carbon monoxide. They decided then to go back to the apartment and kick the door in, which is maybe what they should have done in the goddamn first place.

There is an old Spanish proverb which, when translated into city slang, goes something like this: *When nobody knows nothing, everybody knows everything.*

Nobody seemed to know nothing about the José Vicente Huerta assault. He had been attacked in broad daylight on a clear day by four men carrying sawed-off broom handles, and they had beaten him severely enough to have broken both his legs and opened a dozen or more wounds on his face, but nobody seemed to have had a good look at them, even though the beating had lasted a good five minutes or more.

Delgado was not a natural cynic, but he certainly had his doubts about this one. He went through Huerta's building talking to the tenants on each floor, and then he went to the candy store across the street, from which the front stoop of the building was clearly visible, and talked to the proprietor there, but nobody knew nothing. He decided to try another tack.

There was a junkie hooker in the *barrio*, a nineteen-year-old girl who had only one arm. Her handicap, rather than repelling any prospective customers, seemed instead to excite them wildly. From far and wide, the panting Johns came uptown seeking the One-Armed Bandit, as she was notoriously known. She was more familarly known as Blanca Diaz to those neighbourhood men who were among her regular customers, she having a habit as long as the River Harb, and they knowing a good lay when they stumbled across it, one-armed or not, especially since the habit caused her to charge bargain rates most of the time. Conversely, many of the neighbourhood men were familiarly known to Blanca, and it was for this reason alone that Delgado sought her out.

Blanca was not too terribly interested in passing the time of day with a cop, Puerto Rican or otherwise. But she knew that most of the precinct detectives, unlike Vice Squad cops, were inclined to look the other way where she was concerned, perhaps because of her infirmity. Moreover, she had just had her 3 PM fix and was feeling no pain when Delgado approached her. She was, in fact, enjoying the October sunshine, sitting on a bench on one of the grassy ovals running up the centre of The Stem. She spotted Delgado from the corner of her eye, debated moving, thought *Oh, the hell with it*, and sat where she was, basking.

'Hello, Blanca,' Delgado said.

'Hullo,' she answered.

'You okay?'

'I'm fine. I'm not holding, if that's what you mean.'

'That's not what I mean.'

'I mean, if you're looking for a cheap dope bust . . .'

'I'm not.'

'Okay,' Blanca said, and nodded. She was not an unattractive girl. Her complexion was dark, her hair was black, her eyes a light shade of brown; her lips were perhaps a trifle too full, and there was a small unsightly scar on her jawline, where she had been stabbed by a pimp when she was just sixteen and already shooting heroin three times a day.

'You want to help me?' Delgado asked.

'Doing what?'

'I need some information.'

'I'm no stoolie,' Blanca said.

'If I ask you anything you don't want to answer, you don't have to.'

'Thanks for nothing.'

'*Querida*,' Delgado said, 'we're very nice to you. Be nice back, huh?'

She looked him full in the face, sighed, and said, 'What do you want to know?'

'Everything you know about Joe Huerta.'

'Nothing.'

'He ever come to visit you?'

'Never.'

'What about his partner?'

'Who's his partner?'

'Ray Castañeda.'

'I don't know him,' Blanca said. 'Is he related to Pepe Castañeda?'

'Maybe. Tell me about Pepe.'

Blanca shrugged. 'A punk,' she said.

'How old is he?'

'Thirty? Something like that.'

'What's he do?'

'Who knows? Maybe numbers, I'm not sure. He used to be a junkie years ago, he's one of the few guys I know who kicked it. He was with this street gang, they called themselves the Spanish Nobles or some shit like that, this was when he was still a kid, you know. I was only five or six myself, you know, but he was a very big man in the neighbourhood, rumbling all the time with this wop gang from the other side of the park, I forget the name of the gang, it was a very big one. Then, you know, everybody started doing dope, the guys all lost interest in gang-busting. Pepe was a very big junkie, but he kicked it. I think he went down to Lexington, I'm not sure. Or maybe he just got busted and sent away and kicked it cold turkey, I'm not sure. But he's off it now, I know that.' She shrugged. 'He's still a punk, though.'

'Have you seen him lately?'

'Yeah, he's around all the time. You always see him on the stoop someplace. Always with a bunch of kids around him, you know, listening to his crap. Big man. The reformed whore,' Blanca said, and snorted.

'Have you seen him today?'

'No. I just come down a little while ago. I had a trick with me all night.'

'Where can I find him, would you know?'

'Pepe or the trick?' Blanca asked, and smiled.

'Pepe,' Delgado said, and did not smile back.

'There's a pool hall on Ainsley,' Blanca said. 'He hangs around there a lot.'

'Let's get back to Huerta for a minute, okay?'

'Why?' Blanca asked, and turned to look at a bus that was rumbling up the avenue.

'Because we got away from him too fast,' Delgado said.

'I hardly know him,' Blanca said. She was still watching the bus. Its blue-grey exhaust fumes seemed to fascinate her.

'You mind looking at me?' Delgado said.

She turned back towards him sharply. 'I told you I'm not a stoolie,' Blanca said. 'I don't want to answer no questions about Joe Huerta.'

'Why not? What's he into?'

'No comment.'

'Dope?'

'No comment.'

'Yes or no, Blanca? We know where you live, we can have the Vice Squad banging on your door every ten minutes. Tell me about Huerta.'

'Okay, he's dealing, okay?'

'I thought he had a real estate business.'

'Sure. He's got an acre of land in Mexico, and he grows pot on it.'

'Is he pushing the hard stuff, too?'

'No. Only grass.'

'Does his partner know this?'

'I don't know what his partner knows or don't know. I'm not his partner. Go ask his partner.'

'Maybe I will,' Delgado said. 'After I talk to his partner's brother.'

'You going to look for Pepe now?'

'Yes.'

'Tell him he still owes me five bucks.'

'What for?'

'What do you think for?' Blanca asked.

*   *   *

Genero was waiting on the sidewalk when Willis came out of the phone booth.

'What'd they say?' he asked.

'Nothing yet. They've got a lot of stuff ahead of what we sent them.'

'So how we supposed to know if it's grass or oregano?' Genero said.

'I guess we wait. They told me to call back in a half-hour or so.'

'Those guys at the lab give me a pain in the ass,' Genero said.

'Yeah, well, what're you gonna do?' Willis said. 'We all have our crosses to bear.' The truth was that Genero gave *him* a pain in the ass. They had arranged for pickup and delivery to the lab of the plastic bag full of oregano/marijuana and had asked for a speedy report on it. But the lab was swamped with such requests every day of the week, the average investigating officer never being terribly certain about a suspect drug until it was checked out downtown. Willis had been willing to wait for the report; Genero had insisted that he call the lab and find out what was happening. Now, at twenty minutes to four, they knew what was happening: nothing. So now Genero was beginning to sulk, and Willis was beginning to wish he would go home and explain to his mother how tough it was to be a working detective in this city.

They were in an area of the Quarter that was not as chic as the section farther south, lacking its distinctive Left Bank flair, but boasting of the same high rentals none the less, this presumably because of its proximity to all the shops and theatres and coffee-houses. 3541 Carrier Avenue was a brownstone in a row of identical brownstones worn shoddy by the passage of time. They found a nameplate for Robert Hamling in one of the mailboxes in the entrance hallway downstairs. Willis rang the bell for Apartment 22. An answering buzz on the inner door sounded almost immediately. Genero opened the door and both men moved into a dim ground-floor landing. A flight of steps was directly ahead of them. The building smelled of Lysol. They went up to the second floor, searched for Apartment 22, listened outside the door, heard nothing, and knocked.

'Bobby?' a girl's voice said.

'Police officers,' Willis said.

'What do you want?' the girl asked.

'Open the door,' Genero said.

There was silence inside the apartment. They kept listening. They knew that Robert Hamling wasn't in there with the girl, because the first word out of her mouth had been 'Bobby?' But nobody knows better than cops that the female is the deadlier of the species, and so they waited apprehensively for her to unlock the door, their coats open, their guns within ready drawing distance. When the door finally opened, they were looking at a teenage girl wearing dungarees and a tie-dyed T-shirt. Her face was round, her eyes were blue, her brown hair was long and matted.

'Yes, what do you want?' she said. She seemed very frightened and very nervous. She kept one hand on the doorknob. The other fluttered at the throat of the T-shirt.

'We're looking for Robert Hamling,' Willis said. 'Does he live here?'

'Yes,' she said, tentatively.

'Is he home?'

'No.'

'When do you expect him?'

'I don't know.'

'What's your name, miss?' Genero asked.

'Sonia.'

'Sonia what?'

'Sonia Sobolev.'

'How old are you, Sonia?'

'Seventeen.'

'Do you live here?'

'No.'

'Where *do* you live?'

'In Riverhead.'

'What are you doing here?'

'Waiting for Bobby. He's a friend of mine.'

'When did he go out?'

'I don't know.'

'How'd you get in here?'

'I have a key.'

'Mind if we come in and wait with you?'

'I don't care,' she said, and shrugged. 'If you want to come in, come in.' She stood aside. She was still very frightened. As they entered, she looked past them into the hallway, as if anxious for Hamling to appear and wishing it would be damn soon. Willis caught this, though Genero did not. She closed the door behind them, and together they went into a room furnished with several battered easy chairs, a foam rubber sofa, and a low, slatted coffee table. 'Well, sit down,' she said.

The detectives sat on the sofa. Sonia took one of the chairs opposite them.

'How well do you know Robert Hamling?' Willis asked.

'Pretty well.'

'When did you see him last?'

'Oh ...' she said, and shrugged, and seemed to be thinking it over.

'Yes?'

'Well, what difference does it make?'

'It might make a difference.'

'Last week sometime, I guess.'

'*When* last week?'

'Well, why don't you ask Bobby when he gets here?'

'We will,' Genero said. 'Meantime, we're asking you. When did you see him last?'

'I don't remember,' Sonia said.

'Do you know anybody named Lewis Scott?' Willis asked.

'No.'

'Ever hear of a clothing store called The Monkey Wrench?'

'Yes, I think so.'

'Ever buy any clothes there?'

'I don't remember.'

'Ever buy a black silk blouse there?' Genero asked.

'I don't remember.'

'Show her the blouse, Dick,' Willis said.

Genero produced the manila envelope again. He took the blouse from it and handed it to the girl. 'This yours?' he asked.

'I don't know.'

'Yes or no?' Genero said.

'It could be, I can't tell for sure. I have a lot of clothes.'

'Do you have a lot of black silk blouses bought at a store called The Monkey Wrench?'

'Well, no, but a person could get confused about her clothes. I mean, it's a black silk blouse, it could be *any* black silk blouse. How do I know it's mine?'

'What size blouse do you take?'

'Thirty-four.'

'This is a thirty-four,' Willis said.

'That still doesn't make it mine, does it?' Sonia asked.

'Were you here in Isola last night?' Willis asked.

'Well, yes.'

'Where?'

'Oh, banking around.'

'Where?'

'Here and there.'

'Here and there *where*?'

'You don't have to answer him, Sonia,' a voice from the doorway said, and both detectives turned simultaneously. The boy standing there was about eighteen, with long blond hair and a handlebar moustache. He had on blue jeans and a blue corduroy shirt, over which he wore an open coat with white fur showing on the inside.

'Mr Hamling, I presume,' Willis said.

'That's me,' Hamling said. He turned to close the entrance door. A bright orange, radiating sun was painted on the back of the coat.

'We've been looking for you,' Willis said.

'So now you found me,' Hamling said. 'This is about Lew, isn't it?'

'You tell *us*,' Genero said.

'Sure, it's about Lew,' Hamling said. 'I figured you'd get to me sooner or later.'

'What about him?'

'He jumped out the window last night.'

'Were you there when he jumped?'

'We were *both* there,' Hamling said, and glanced at the girl. The girl nodded.

'Want to tell us what happened?'

'He was on a bum trip,' Hamling said. 'He thought he could fly. I tried to hold him down, but he ran for the window and jumped out. End of story.'

'Why didn't you report this to the police?'

'What for? I've got long hair.'

Willis sighed. 'Well,' he said, 'we're here now, so why don't you just tell us everything that happened, and we'll file the damn report and close out the case.'

Genero looked at him. Willis was taking out his pad. 'Want to tell me what time you went over there?'

'It must've been about four-thirty or so. Look,' Hamling said, 'am I gonna get in any trouble on this?'

'Why should you? If Scott jumped out the window, that's suicide, plain and simple.'

'Yeah, well he did.'

'Okay, so help us close it out, will you? This is a headache for us, too,' Willis said, and again Genero looked at him. 'What happened when you got there?'

'Why do *I* have to be in it, that's all I want to know?' Hamling said.

'Well, you *were* in it, weren't you?'

'Yeah, but . . .'

'So what are we supposed to do? Make believe you *weren't* there? Come on, give us a break. Nobody's trying to get you in trouble. You know how many acid freaks jump out the window every day of the week?'

'I just don't want it to get in the papers or anything,'

Hamling said. 'That's why I didn't call you in the first place.'

'We realize that,' Willis said. 'We'll do everything we can to protect you. Just give us the information we need to get a report typed up, that's all.'

'Well, okay,' Hamling said reluctantly.

'So what happened? Did all three of you go up there together, or what?' Willis said.

'No, I ran into him on the street,' Hamling said. 'I was alone at the time. I called Sonia up later, and she came over.'

Willis was writing on the pad. Genero was still watching him. Genero had the strangest feeling that something was going on, but he didn't know quite what. He also had the feeling that he was about to learn something. He was both confused and somewhat exhilarated. He kept his mouth shut and simply watched and listened. 'All right,' Willis said, 'you ran into this friend of yours and . . .'

'No, no, he wasn't a friend of mine,' Hamling said.

'You didn't know him?'

'No, I just ran into him in this coffee joint, and we began talking, you know? So he asked me if I wanted to come up to his place and hear some records, you know, and . . . listen, can I get in trouble if I *really* level with you guys?'

'I'd appreciate it if you would,' Willis said.

'Well, he said he had some good stuff and maybe we could have a smoke. That's all I thought it was at the time. Just a smoke, you see. I mean, if I'd known the guy had acid in his apartment . . .'

'You didn't know that at the time?'

'No, hell, no. I usually try to stay away from these plastic hippies, anyway, they're usually a lot of trouble.'

'How do you mean, trouble?'

'Oh, you know, they're trying to show off all the time, trying to be something they really aren't. Weekend hippies, plastic hippies, same damn thing. None of them are *really* making the scene, they're only *pretending* to make it.'

'How about you?'

'I consider myself genuine,' Hamling said with dignity.

'How about Sonia?'

'Well, she's sort of a weekend hippie,' Hamling said, 'but she's also a very groovy chick, so I put up with her.' He smiled broadly. Sonia did not smile back. She was still frightened. Her hands were clasped in her lap, and she kept shifting her eyes from Willis to Hamling as though knowing that a dangerous game was being played, and wanting desperately to be elsewhere. Genero sensed this, and also sensed in his inexperienced, newly promoted way that the girl was Willis' real prey and that it would only be a matter of time before he sprang for her jugular. The girl knew this, too. Hamling seemed to be the only person in the room who did *not* know it. Supremely confident of himself, he plunged on.

'Anyway, we went up there and smoked a few joints and drank some wine, and it was then I suggested I give Sonia a ring and have her come over, join in the celebration.'

'What were you celebrating?' Willis asked.

Hamling hesitated. He thought the question over for several moments, and then grinned and said, 'Life. Living. Being alive.'

'Okay,' Willis said.

Genero was still watching very closely, learning as he went along. He knew, for example, that Hamling had just told a lie. Whatever they'd been celebrating, it had not been life or living or being alive. He could not have told *how* he knew Hamling had lied, but he knew it. And Willis knew it. And the girl knew it. And Genero knew that before long Willis would come back to the reason for the celebration, in an attempt to expose Hamling's lie. Genero felt great. He felt as though he were watching a cops-and-robbers movie on television. He didn't want it to end, ever. It never once occurred to him, as he watched and listened to Willis, that he himself was a detective. All he knew was that he was having a great time. He almost asked the girl how she was enjoying herself. He wished he had a bag of popcorn.

'So I went down to the street,' Hamling said. 'He didn't

have a phone in the apartment. I went to a pay phone to call Sonia. She ...'

'Where was Sonia?'

'Here. I was supposed to meet her here at seven o'clock, and this was now maybe close to eight. She has a key, so I knew she'd let herself in.'

'*Was* she here?'

'Oh, yeah. So I asked her to meet me uptown. She said she wasn't too familiar with that part of the city, so I told her what train to take, and I met her at the subway stop.'

'What time was that?'

'She must've got there about eight-thirty. Wouldn't you say it was eight-thirty, Sonia?'

The girl nodded.

'Did you go back to the apartment then?'

'Yes,' Hamling said. 'That was the *first* mistake.'

'Why?'

'He was naked when he opened the door. I thought at first ... hell, I didn't know *what* to think. Then I realized he was high. And then I realized he was on an acid trip. A bummer. I tried to find out what he'd dropped, there's all kinds of stuff, you know, good and bad. Like there's a whole lot of difference between white owsley and green flats; you get shit with strychnine and arsenic mixed into it, man, that's bad news. But he wasn't making any sense at all, didn't know what he'd dropped, didn't know where he was, kept running around the room bare-assed and screaming and yelling he could fly. Scared Sonia half out of her mind, right, honey?'

The girl nodded.

'When did he jump out the window?' Willis asked.

'I don't know, we must've been there maybe twenty minutes. I was trying to talk him down, you know, telling him to cool it, calm it, like that, when all of a sudden he jumps up and makes a break for the window. I tried to grab him, but I was too late. The window was closed, you dig? He went through it head first, man oh man. I looked down in the yard, and there he was laying there like ...' Hamling shook his head.

'So what'd you do?'

'I grabbed Sonia, and we split. I didn't want to get mixed up in it. You got long hair, you're dead.'

'Well, looks open and shut to me,' Willis said, and closed his pad. 'What do you think, Dick?'

Genero nodded. 'Yeah, looks open and shut to me, too,' he said. He was beginning to think he'd been mistaken about Willis. Was it possible his more experienced partner had *really* only been after the details of a suicide? He felt vaguely disappointed.

'Just one more question, I guess,' Willis said, 'and then we can leave you alone. Can't thank you enough for your cooperation. People just don't realize how much trouble they cause when they decide to kill themselves.'

'Oh, I can imagine,' Hamling said.

'We have to treat suicides just like homicides, you know. Same people to notify, same reports to fill out, it's a big job.'

'Oh, sure,' Hamling said.

'Well, thanks again,' Willis said, and started for the door. 'Coming, Dick?'

'Yep,' Genero said, and nodded. 'Thanks a lot,' he said to Hamling.

'Glad to be of help,' Hamling said. 'If I'd known you guys were going to be so decent, I wouldn't have split, I mean it.'

'Oh, that last question,' Willis said, as though remembering something that had momentarily slipped his mind. 'Miss Sobolev . . .'

Hamling's eyes darted to the girl.

'Miss Sobolev, did you take off your blouse before or after Scott jumped out the window?'

'I don't remember,' she said.

'I guess it was before,' Willis said. 'Because you both left immediately after he jumped.'

'Yes, I suppose it was before,' Sonia said.

'Miss Sobolev . . . *why* did you take off your blouse?'

'Well . . . I don't know why, really. I mean, I guess I just felt like taking it off.'

'I guess she took it off because . . .'

'Well, let's let *her* answer it, okay? So we can clear this up, and leave you alone, okay? Why'd you take it off, Miss Sobolev?'

'I guess it was . . . I guess it was warm in the apartment.'

'So you took off your blouse?'

'Yes.'

'You'd never met Scott before, but you took off your blouse . . .'

'Well, it was warm.'

'He was on a bum trip, running around the place and screaming, and you decided to take off your blouse.'

'Yes.'

'Mmm,' Willis said. 'Do you want to know how *I* read this, Mr Hamling?'

'How?' Hamling said, and looked at the girl. Genero looked at both of them, and then looked at Willis. He didn't know *what* was going on. He was so excited, he almost wet his pants.

'I think you're protecting the girl,' Willis said.

'Yeah?' Hamling said, puzzled.

'Yeah. It's my guess they were balling in that apartment, and something happened, and the girl here shoved Scott out the window, that's my guess.' The girl's mouth had fallen open. Willis turned to her and nodded. 'We're going to have to take you with us, Miss Sobolev.'

'What do you . . . *mean*?' she said.

'Uptown,' Willis answered. 'Mr Hamling, we won't be needing you for now, but the District Attorney may want to ask some more questions after we've booked Miss Sobolev. Please don't leave the city without informing us of your . . .'

'Hey, *wait* a minute,' the girl said.

'You want to get your coat, please?' Willis said.

'Listen, *I* didn't push anybody out that damn window!' she said, standing suddenly and putting her hands on her hips.

'Scott was naked, you had your blouse off, what do you expect?...'

'That was *his* idea!' Sonia shouted, hurling the words at Hamling.

'Cool it, Sonia,' Hamling warned.

'It was *his* idea to get undressed, he wanted to find the damn...'

'The damn *what*?' Willis snapped.

'The damn money belt!'

Hamling was breaking for the front door. Genero watched in fascinated immobility. Willis was directly in Hamling's path, between him and the door. Hamling was a head taller than Willis and a foot wider, and Genero was certain the boy would now knock his partner flat on his ass. He almost wished he would, because then it would be terribly exciting to see what happened next. Hamling was charging for that front door like an express train, and Genero fully expected him to bowl Willis over and continue running into the corridor, down the steps, into the street, and all the way to China. If he was in Willis' place, he would have got out of the way very quickly, because a man can get hurt by a speeding locomotive. But instead of getting out of the way, Willis started running *towards* Hamling, and suddenly dropped to his right knee. Hamling's right foot was ahead of his left at that moment, with all the weight on it, and as he rushed forward, Willis grabbed his left ankle, and began pulling Hamling forward and pushing him upward at the same time, his right hand against Hamling's chest as he rose. The result was somewhat similar to a football quarterback being hit high and low at the same instant from two opposite directions. Hamling flew over backward, his ankle still clutched in Willis' hand, his head banging back hard against the door. Genero blinked.

Willis was stooping over the fallen Hamling now, a gun in his right hand, his handcuffs open in the other hand. He slapped one onto Hamling's wrist, squeezed it closed. The sawtooth edges clicked shut into the retaining metal of the receiver. Willis pulled hard on the cuffs and yanked

Hamling to his feet. He whirled him around, pulled his other arm behind his back, and snapped the second cuff shut.

Genero was out of breath.

Danny Gimp was a stool pigeon who told everybody he was a burglar. This was understandable. In a profession where access to underworld gossip was absolutely essential, it was a decided advantage to be considered one of the boys.

Actually, Danny was not a burglar, even though he had been arrested and convicted for burglary in the city of Los Angeles, California, back in the year nineteen hundred and thirty-eight. He had always been a sickly person, and had gone out West to cure himself of a persistent cold. He had met a drinking companion in a bar on La Brea, and the guy had asked Danny to stop by his house while he picked up some more money so that they could continue their all-night revel. They had driven up the Strip past La Cienega and had both entered the guy's house through the back door. The guy had gone into the bedroom and come back a little while later to where Danny was waiting for him in the kitchen. He had picked up several hundred dollars in cash, not to mention a diamond and ruby necklace valued at forty-seven thousand five hundred dollars. But it seemed that Danny was not the only person waiting for his drinking companion to come out of the bedroom. The Los Angeles police were also waiting. In fact, the way Danny found out about the value of the necklace was that the police happened to tell him. Danny tried to explain all this to the judge. He also mentioned to the judge that he had suffered polio as a child, and was a virtual cripple, and that jail would not be very good for his health or his disposition. The judge had kindly considered everything Danny had to say and then had sentenced Danny and his drinking companion to a minimum of five and a maximum of ten. Danny never spoke to his drinking companion again after that night, even though the men were in the same cell block. The guy was killed by a black homosexual prisoner a year later, stabbed in the throat with a table knife honed to razor sharpness in the sheet metal shop. The black homosexual stood trial for murder, was convicted, and was executed. Danny served his time thinking about the vagaries of justice, and left prison with the single qualification he would need to pursue a profitable career as a snitch. He was an ex-con. If you can't trust an ex-con, who *can* you trust? Such was the underworld belief, and it accounted for the regularity with which Danny Gimp received choice bits of information, which he then passed on to the police at a price. It was a living, and not a bad one.

Carl Kapek had put in a call to Danny that afternoon. The two men met in Grover Park at seven minutes before five. The afternoon was beginning to wane. They sat together on a park bench and watched governesses wheeling their charges home in baby buggies, watched touch football games beginning to break up, watched a little girl walking slowly by on the winding path, trailing a skip rope behind her and studying the ground the way only little girls can, with an intense concentration that indicated she was pondering all the female secrets of the universe.

'Belinda, huh?' Danny said.

'Yeah, Belinda.'

Danny sniffed. He always seemed to have a cold lately, Kapek noticed. Maybe he was getting old.

'And you don't know Belinda *what*, huh?' Danny said.

'That's why I called you,' Kapek said.

'She's a spade, huh?'

'Yeah.'

'I don't read her right off,' Danny said. He sniffed again. 'It's getting to be winter already, you realize that?'

'It's not so bad,' Kapek said.

'It stinks,' Danny answered. 'Why do you want this broad?'

'She mugged a marine.'

'You're putting me on,' Danny said, and laughed.

'She didn't do it alone.'

'A guy was in it with her?'

'Yeah. She played up to the marine in a bar on Seventeenth, indicated she wanted him to follow her. When he did, she led him to her partner, and they put him out of action.'

'Is the guy a spade, too?'

'No, he's white.'

'Belinda,' Danny said. 'That's a pretty name. I knew a girl named Belinda once. Only girl I ever knew who didn't mind the leg. This was in Chicago one time. I was in Chicago one time. I got people in Chicago. Belinda Kolacskowska. A Pole. Pretty as a picture, blonde hair, blue eyes, big tits.' Danny demonstrated with his hands, and then immediately put them back in his pockets. 'I asked her one time how come she was going out with a guy like me. I was talking about the limp, you know? She said, "What do you mean, a guy like you?" So I looked her in the eye, and I said, "You know what I mean, Belinda." And she said, "No, I don't know what you mean, Danny." So I said, "Belinda, the fact is that I limp." So she smiled and said, "You *do*?" I'll never forget that smile. I swear to God, if I live to be a hundred and ten, I'll never forget the way Belinda smiled at me that day in Chicago. I felt I could run a mile that day. I felt I could win the goddamn Olympics.' He shook his head, and then sniffed again. A flock of pigeons suddenly took wing not six feet from where the men were sitting, filling the air with the sound of their flight. They soared up against the sky, wheeled, and alighted again near a bench farther on, where an old man in a threadbare brown coat was throwing breadcrumbs into the air.

'Anyway, that ain't the Belinda you're looking for,' Danny said. He thought a moment longer, and then seemed to suppress the memory completely, pulling his head into his overcoat, thrusting his hands deeper into his pockets. 'Can you give me a description of her?' he asked.

'All I know is she's black, and well built, and she was wearing a red dress.'

'That could mean two thousand girls in this city,' Danny said. 'What about the guy?'

'Nothing.'

'Great.'

'What do you think?'

'I think you're very good for a chuckle on a Sunday when winter's coming, that's what I think.'

'Can you help or not?'

'Let me listen a little, who knows? Will you be around?'

'I'll be around.'

'I'll get back.'

There are times in the city when night refuses to come.

The afternoon lingers, the light changes only slowly and imperceptibly, there is a sense of sweet suspension.

This was just such a day.

There was a briskness to the air, you could never confuse this with a spring day. And yet the afternoon possessed that same luminous quality, the sky so intensely blue that it seemed to vibrate indignantly against encroachment, flatly resisting passage through the colour spectrum to darkness. When the street lights came on at five-thirty, they did so in vain. There was nothing to illuminate, the day was still bright. The sun hung stubbornly over the buildings to the west in downtown Majesta and Calm's Point, defying the earth's rotation, balking at extinction behind roof copings and chimney pots. The citizens of the city lingered in the streets bemused, reluctant to go indoors, as though witnessing some vast astronomical disorder, some realized Nostradamus prediction – it would be daytime for ever, the night would never come; there would be dancing in the streets.

The sky to the west yielded at last.

In Herbert Gross' apartment, the light was beginning to fade.

Carella and Brown had been in there for close to three hours now, and whereas they had searched the place from floor to ceiling, wall to wall, timber to toilet tank, they had not found a single clue that told them where Gross had been heading when he hopped that uptown bus.

The clue was everywhere around them. They just hadn't found it yet.

The apartment was a contradiction in itself. It was small and cramped, a cubicle in a crumbling tenement surrounded by warehouses. But it was crowded with furniture that surely had been purchased in the early thirties, when solidity was a virtue and inlaid mahogany was the decorative rule. In the living-room, a huge overstuffed sofa was upholstered in maroon mohair, its claw feet clutching the faded Persian rug that covered the floor. The sofa alone would have been quite enough to overwhelm the dimensions of the small room, but there were two equally overstuffed easy chairs, and a credenza that seemed to have wandered in from an ornate dining-room someplace, and a standing floor lamp with a pink, fringed shade, and an ornately framed painting of snow-clad mountain peaks towering over a placid lake, and a Stromberg-Carlson floor model radio complete with push buttons and a jukebox look, and mahogany end tables on either side of the sofa, each with a tiny drawer, each carrying a huge porcelain lamp with a shade covered in plastic.

The first bedroom had a huge double bed with mahogany headboard and footboard and an unmade mattress. A heavy mahogany dresser of the type that used to be called a 'bureau' when Busby Berkeley was all the rage, complete with its own mahogany-framed mirror, was on the wall opposite the bed. A taller version of it – the male counterpart, so to speak – with longer hanging space for trousers and suits and a row of drawers one atop the other for the storing of handkerchiefs, cuff links, and sundries (Jimmy Walker would have called it a 'chiffonier'), was on the window wall.

The second bedroom was furnished in more modern terms, with two narrow beds covered with simple throws, a Mexican rug hanging on the wall over them. A bookcase was on the wall opposite, alongside a closet without a door. With the exception of the kitchen and the bathroom, there was one other room in the apartment, and this room seemed to have escaped from Arthur Miller's play *The Price*. It was literally packed from floor to ceiling with furniture and china and glassware and marked and unmarked cartons (among those marked was one lettered with the words 'WORLD'S FAIR 1939') and piles of books tied with twine, and cooking utensils, and even old articles of clothing draped over chairs or cartons, a veritable child's dream of an attic hideout, equipped with anything needed to serve whatever imaginary excursion suited the fancy.

'I don't get this place,' Carella said.

'Neither do I,' Brown said. He turned on the floor lamp in the living-room, and they sat opposite each other, tired and dusty, Carella on the monstrous sofa, Brown in one of the big easy chairs. The room was washed with the glow of the pink, fringed lampshade. Carella almost felt as if he were sitting down to do his homework to the accompaniment of 'Omar the Mystic' flooding from the old Stromberg-Carlson.

'Everything's wrong but that one bedroom,' he said. 'The rest of it doesn't fit.'

'Or maybe vice versa,' Brown said.

'I mean, who the hell has furniture like that nowadays?'

'My mother has furniture like that,' Brown said.

Both men were silent. It was Carella who broke the silence at last.

'When did Goldenthal's mother die?' he asked.

'Three months ago, I think the report said. He was living with her until then.'

'You think all this crap might have been hers?'

'Maybe. Maybe he moved it all here when he left the other apartment.'

'You remember her first name?'

'Minnie.'

'How many Goldenthals do you suppose there are in the telephone book?'

They did not even consider looking in the directories for Bethtown, Majesta, or Calm's Point, because Gross had been heading *uptown*, and access to all those other sections of the city would have required going *downtown*. They did not consider looking in the Riverhead directory, either, because

Gross had taken a bus, and bus transportation all the way to
Riverhead was a hell of a slow way to go, when there were
express trains running all day long. So they limited their
search to the Isola directory alone. (There was one other
reason they consulted just this one phone book; it happened
to be the *only* one Gross had in the apartment.)

There were eight Goldenthals listed in the Isola directory.

But only one of them was Minnie Goldenthal – now de-
ceased, poor lady, her name surviving in print only until
next year's directory would be published by the telephone
company.

Sic transit gloria mundi.

The building in which Minnie Goldenthal had lived was a
twelve-storey yellow brick structure bristling with television
antennae. It was fronted by a small cement courtyard
flanked by two yellow brick pillars, atop which sat two stone
urns that were probably planted with flowers in the spring,
but that now contained only withered stalks. Enclosing this
courtyard were the two wings of the building, and a row of
apartments connecting both wings, so that the result was an
architectural upside-down U facing the low flat entrance
steps to the courtyard. The mailboxes for each wing were in
the entryway to the right and left. Carella checked one
entry, Brown the other. There was no listing for Goldenthal,
Minnie or otherwise.

'What do you think?' Carella asked.

'Let's check the super,' Brown suggested.

The superintendent lived on the ground floor, in an apartment behind the staircase. He came to the door in his undershirt. A television set was going somewhere in his
apartment, but apparently the show had not completely captured his attention, because he was carrying the Sunday
comics in his right hand. The detectives identified themselves. The super looked at Carella's shield. He looked at
Carella's ID card. Then he said, 'Yes?'

'Was there a Minnie Goldenthal living here recently?'
Carella asked.

The super listened attentively to his every word, as though he were being asked a question which, if answered correctly would cause him to win a hundred-thousand-dollar jackpot.

Then he said, 'Yes.'

'Which apartment?'

'Nine D.'

'Anyone living in that apartment now?'

'Son's still living in it.'

'Bernie Goldenthal?'

'That's right. Don't know *why* he's living in it, mind you. Moved all the furniture out a little while after Minnie died. Still pays the rent, though.' The super shrugged. 'Tell you the truth, the owners wish he'd get out. That apartment's price-fixed. Nice big old apartment. If he gets out, they can put a new tenant in and legally raise the rent.'

'Anybody up there now?' Carella asked.

'Don't know,' the super said. 'Don't keep tabs on the comings and goings of the people who live here. Their business is their business, and mine is mine.'

'Law requires you to have a key to all the apartments in the dwelling,' Carella said. 'Have you got one for Nine D?'

'Yep.'

'All right if we use it?'

'What for?'

'To enter the apartment.'

'That's illegal, ain't it?'

'We won't tell anybody if you won't,' Brown said.

'Well,' the super said, and shrugged. 'Okay,' he said, and shrugged again. 'I guess.'

Carella and Brown took the elevator up to the ninth floor and stepped into the corridor. Neither man said a word to the other, but both simultaneously drew their revolvers. 9D was at the far end of the hall. They listened outside the door and heard nothing. Cautiously, Carella inserted the passkey into the lock. He nodded to Brown, and twisted the key. There was only a small click as the lock turned, but it must have sounded like a warning shot inside that apartment. Carella and Brown burst into a long narrow entrance foyer. At the far end of the foyer, they saw Herbert Gross and a blond man they assumed to be Bernard Goldenthal, both of them armed.

'Hold it right there!' Carella shouted, but neither of the two men were holding anything right there or right anywhere. They opened fire just as Carella and Brown threw themselves flat on the linoleum-covered floor. Goldenthal made a break for a doorway to the right of the long foyer. Brown shouted a warning and fired almost before the words left his lips. The slug caught Goldenthal in the leg, knocked him off his feet and sent him flailing against the corridor wall, where he slid to the floor. Gross held his ground, firing down the long length of the foyer, pulling off shot after shot until his pistol clicked empty. He was reaching into his jacket pocket, presumably for fresh cartridges, when Carella shouted, 'Move and you're dead!'

Gross' hand stopped in mid-motion. He squinted down the corridor, silhouetted in the light that spilled from the room Goldenthal had tried to reach.

'Drop the gun,' Carella said.

Gross did not move.

'*Drop* it!' Carella shouted. 'Now!'

'You, too, Goldie!' Brown shouted.

Goldenthal and Gross – one crouched against the wall clutching his bleeding leg, the other with his hand still hanging motionless over his jacket pocket – exchanged quick glances. Without saying a word to each other, they dropped their guns to the floor. Gross kicked them away as if they were contaminated. The guns came spinning down the length of the corridor one after the other, sliding along the waxed linoleum.

Carella got to his feet, and started towards the two men. Behind him, Brown was crouched on one knee, his gun resting on his forearm and pointing directly at the far end of the foyer. Carella threw Gross against the wall, quickly frisked him, and then bent over Goldenthal.

'Okay,' he called to Brown, and then glanced into the

room on the right of the foyer. It, too, was loaded with household goods. But unlike the stuff in the apartment downtown, this had not come from a dead woman's home, this was not the accumulation of a lifetime. This was, instead, the result of God knew how many recent burglaries and robberies, a veritable storehouse of television sets, radios, typewriters, tape recorders, broilers, mixers, luggage, you name it, right down to a complete set of the Encyclopaedia Britannica – a criminal bargain basement, awaiting only the services of a good fence.

'Nice little place you've got here,' Carella said, and then handcuffed Gross to Goldenthal and Goldenthal to the radiator. From a telephone on the kitchen wall, the late Minnie's last shopping list still tacked up beside it, he called the station house and asked for a meat wagon. It arrived at exactly 6 PM, not seven minutes after Carella requested it. By that time, Goldenthal had spilled a goodly amount of blood all over his mother's linoleum.

'I'm bleeding to death here,' he complained to one of the hospital orderlies who was lifting him onto the stretcher.

'That's the least of your worries,' the orderly answered.

Delgado had not found Pepe Castañeda in the pool hall, nor had he found him in any one of a dozen bars he tried in the neighbourhood. It was now a quarter past six, and he was about ready to give up the search. On the dubious assumption, however, that a pool shooter might also be a bowler, he decided to hit the Ponce Bowling Lanes on Culver Avenue before heading back to the squad-room.

The place was on the second floor of an old brick building. Delgado went up the narrow flight of steps and came into a fluorescent-lighted room with a counter just opposite the entrance doorway. A bald-headed man was sitting on a stool behind the counter, reading a newspaper. He looked up as Delgado came in, went back to the newspaper, finished the story he was reading, and then put both hands flat on the countertop. 'All the alleys are full,' he said. 'You got maybe a half-hour wait.'

'I don't want an alley,' Delgado said.

The man behind the counter looked at him more carefully, decided he was a cop, gave a brief knowledgeable nod, but said nothing.

'I'm looking for a man named Pepe Castañeda. Is he here?'

'What do you want him for?' the man said.

'I'm a police officer,' Delgado said, and flashed the tin. 'I want to ask him some questions.'

'I don't want no trouble here,' the man said.

'Why should there be trouble? Is Castañeda trouble?'

'*He's* not the trouble,' the man said, and looked at Delgado meaningfully.

'Neither am I,' Delgado said. 'Where is he?'

'Lane number five,' the man said.

'Thanks.'

Delgado went through the doorway adjacent to the counter and found himself in a larger room than the small reception area had promised. There were twelve alleys in all, each of them occupied with bowlers. A bar was at the far end of the place, with tables and chairs set up around it. A jukebox was playing a rock-and-roll song. The record ended as Delgado moved past the racks of bowling balls against the low wall that separated the lanes from the area behind them. A Spanish-language song erupted from the loudspeakers. Everywhere, there was the reverberating clamour of falling pins, multiplied and echoing in the high-ceilinged room, joined by voices raised in jubilant exclamation or disgruntled invective.

There were four men bowling in lane number five. Three of them were seated on the leatherette banquette that formed a semicircle around the score pad. The fourth man stood waiting for his ball to return. It came rolling down the tracks from the far end of the alley, hit the stop mechanism, eased its way towards his waiting hand. He picked up the ball, stepped back some five feet from the foul line, crouched, started his forward run, right arm coming back, left arm out for balance, stopped dead and released the ball.

It curved down the alley and arced in true between the one and three pins. The bowler hung frozen in motion, his right arm still extended, left arm back, crouched and waiting for the explosion of pins. They flew into the air like gleeful cheer-leaders, there was the sound of their leap as the ball sent them helter-skelter, the additional sound of their pell-mell return to the polished alley floor. The bowler shouted, 'Made it!' and turned to the three men on the banquette.

'Which one of you is Pepe Castañeda?' Delgado asked.

The bowler, who was walking back towards the score pad to supervise the correct marking of the strike, stopped in his tracks and looked up at Delgado. He was a short man with straight black hair and pockmarked face, thin with the light step of a dancer, a step that seemed even airier in the red, rubber-soled bowling shoes.

'I'm Castañeda,' he said. 'Who're you?'

'Detective Delgado, Eighty-seventh Squad,' Delgado said. 'Mind if I ask you a few questions?'

'What about?'

'Is Ramon Castañeda your brother?'

'That's right.'

'Why don't we walk over there and talk a little?'

'Over where?'

'The tables there.'

'I'm in the middle of a game.'

'The game can wait.'

Castañeda shrugged. One of the men on the banquette said, 'Go ahead, Pepe. We'll order a round of beer mean-while.'

'How many frames we got to go?'

'Just three,' the other man said.

'This gonna take long?' Castañeda asked.

'I don't think so,' Delgado said.

'Well, okay. We're ahead here, I don't want to cool off.'

They walked together to the bar at the far end of the room. Two young girls in tight slacks were standing near the jukebox, pondering their next selection. Castañeda looked them over, and then pulled out a chair at one of the tables.

The men sat opposite each other. The jukebox erupted again with sound. The intermittent rumble of exploding pins was a steady counterpoint.

'What do you want to know?' Castañeda asked.

'Your brother's got a partner named José Huerta,' Delgado said.

'That's right.'

'Do you know him?'

'Yeah, I know Joe.'

'Do you know he was beaten up this morning?'

'He was? No, I didn't know that. You got a cigarette? I left mine on the table back there.'

'I don't smoke,' Delgado said.

'I didn't used to smoke, either,' Castañeda said. 'But, you know ...' He shrugged. 'You break one habit, you pick up another, huh?' He grinned. The grin was wide and infectious. He was perhaps three or four years younger than Delgado, but he suddenly looked like a teenager. 'I used to be a junkie, you know. Did you know that?'

'Yes, I've heard it.'

'I kicked it.'

'I've heard that, too.'

'Ain't you impressed?'

'I'm impressed,' Delgado said.

'So am I,' Castañeda said, and grinned again. Delgado grinned with him. 'So, I still don't know what you want from me,' Castañeda said.

'He got beat up pretty badly,' Delgado said. 'Broke both his legs, chopped his face up like hamburger.'

'Gee, that's too bad,' Castañeda said. 'Who done it?'

'Four men.'

'Boy,' Castañeda said, and shook his head.

'They got him on the front stoop of his building. He was on his way to church.'

'Yeah? Where does he live?'

'On South Sixth.'

'Oh yeah, that's right,' Castañeda said. 'Across the street from the candy store, right?'

'Yes. The reason I wanted to talk to you,' Delgado said, 'is that your brother seemed to think the four men who beat up Huerta were *asked* to beat him up.'

'I don't follow you,' Castañeda said.

'When I asked your brother who disliked Huerta, he said, "No one dislikes him enough to have him beaten up." '

'So? What does that mean?'

'It means . . .'

'It don't mean nothing,' Castañeda said, and shrugged.

'It means your brother thinks the men who beat up Huerta were doing it for somebody else, not themselves.'

'I don't see where you get that,' Castañeda said. 'That was just a way of speaking, that's all. My brother didn't mean nothing by it.'

'Let's say he did. Let's say for the moment that somebody *wanted* Huerta beaten up. And let's say he asked four men to do the favour for him.'

'Okay, let's say that.'

'Would you happen to know who those four men might be?'

'Nope,' Castañeda said. 'I really could use a cigarette, you know? You mind if I go back to the table for them?'

'The cigarette can wait, Pepe. There's a man in the hospital with two broken legs and a busted face.'

'Gee, that's too bad,' Castañeda said, 'but maybe the man should've been more careful, you know? Then maybe nobody would've *wanted* him beaten up, and nobody would've talked to anybody *about* beating him up.'

'Who wanted him hurt, Pepe?'

'You interested in some guesses?'

'I'm interested.'

'Joe's a pusher, did you know that?'

'I know that.'

'Grass. For now. But I never yet met a guy selling grass who didn't later figure there was more profit in the hard stuff. It's just a matter of time, that's all.'

'So?'

'So maybe somebody didn't like the idea of him poisoning

the neighbourhood, you dig? I'm only saying. But it's something to consider, right?'

'Yes, it's something to consider.'

'And maybe Joe was chasing after somebody's wife, too. Maybe somebody's got a real pretty wife, and maybe Joe's been making it with her, you dig? That's another thing to consider. So maybe somebody decided to break both his legs so he couldn't run around no more balling somebody else's wife and selling poison to the kids in the *barrio*. And maybe they decided to mess up his face for good measure, you dig? So he wouldn't look so pretty to other guys' wives, and so maybe when he come up to a kid in the neighbourhood and tried to get him hooked, the kid might not want to deal with somebody who had a face looked like it hit a meat grinder.' Castañeda paused. 'Those are all things to consider, right?'

'Yes, they're all things to consider,' Delgado said.

'I don't think you're ever gonna find those guys who beat him up,' Castañeda said. 'But what difference does it make?'

'What do you mean?'

'He got what he deserved. That's justice, ain't it? That's what you guys are interested in, ain't it? Justice?'

'Yes, we're interested in justice.'

'So this was justice,' Castañeda said.

Delgado looked at him.

'Wasn't it?' Castañeda asked.

'Yes, I think it was,' Delgado said. He nodded, rose from the table suddenly, pushed his chair back under it, and said, 'Nice talking to you. See you around.'

'Buy you a drink or something?' Castañeda asked.

'Thanks, I've still got an hour before I'm off duty,' Delgado answered, and walked away from the table.

Behind him, Castañeda raised his hand in farewell.

It was 7 PM by the time Brown finally got around to Mary Ellingham, the lady who had called in twelve hours before to report that her husband was missing. Full darkness was upon the city now, but it was not yet night-time; it was still that time of day called 'evening', a poetic word that always stirred something deep inside Brown, perhaps because he had never heard the word as a child and only admitted it to his vocabulary after he met Connie, his wife-to-be, when things stopped being merely night and day, or black and white; Connie had brought shadings to his life, and for that he would love her for ever.

North Trinity was a two-block-long street off Silvermine Oval, adjacent to fancy Silvermine Road, which bordered on the River Harb and formed the northern frontier of the precinct. From where Brown had parked the car, he could see the waters of the river, and uptown the scattered lights of the estates in Smoke Rise, the brighter illumination on the Hamilton Bridge. The lights were on along Trinity, too, beckoning warmly from windows in the rows of brownstones that faced the secluded street. Brown knew that behind most of those windows, the occupants were enjoying their cocktail hour. One could always determine the socio-economic standing of anybody in this city by asking him what time he ate his dinner. In a slum like Diamondback, the dinner hour had already come and gone. On Trinity Street, the residents were having their before-dinner drinks. Farther uptown in Smoke Rise, the dinner hour would not start until nine or nine-thirty – although the cocktail hour may have started at noon.

Brown was hungry.

There were no lights burning at 742 North Trinity. Brown looked at his watch, shrugged, and rang the front doorbell. He waited, rang the doorbell a second time, and then stepped down off the front stoop to look up at the second storey of the building, where a light had suddenly come on. He went back up the steps and waited. He heard someone approaching the door. A peephole flap was thrown back.

'Yes?' a woman's voice asked.

'Mrs Ellingham?'

'Yes?'

'Detective Brown, Eighty-seventh Squad.'

'Oh,' Mrs Ellingham said. 'Oh, just a minute, please.' The

peephole flap fell back into place. He heard the door being unlocked.

Mary Ellingham was about forty years old. She was wearing a man's flannel robe. Her hair was disarrayed. Her face was flushed.

'I'm sorry I got here so late,' Brown said. 'We had a sort of busy day.'

'Oh,' Mrs Ellingham said. 'Yes.'

'I won't keep you long,' Brown said, reaching into his pocket for his pad and pen. 'If you'll just give me a description of your husband . . .'

'Oh,' Mrs Ellingham said.

'His name is Donald Ellingham, is that correct?'

'Yes, but . . .'

'How old is he?'

'Well, you see . . .'

Brown looked up from his pad. Mrs Ellingham seemed terribly embarrassed all at once. Before she uttered another word, Brown realized what he had walked in on, and he too was suddenly embarrassed.

'You see,' Mrs Ellingham said, 'he's back. My husband. He got back just a little while ago.'

'Oh,' Brown said.

'Yes,' she said.

'Oh.'

'Yes. I'm sorry. I suppose I should have called . . .'

'No, no, that's all right,' Brown said. He put his pad and his pen back into his pocket, and reached behind him for the doorknob. 'Glad he's back, glad everything worked out all right.'

'Yes,' Mrs Ellingham said.

'Goodnight,' Brown said.

'Goodnight,' she said.

She closed the door gently behind him as he went down the steps. Just before he got into his automobile, he glanced back at the building. The upstairs light had already gone out again.

*   *   *

Back at the squad-room, the three detectives who had been called in off vacation were bitching about the speed with which Carella and Brown had cracked the grocery store case. It was one thing to interrupt a man's vacation if there was a goddamn *need* for it; it was another to call him in and trot him around all day asking questions and gathering data while two other guys were out following a hot lead that resulted in an arrest.

'You know what I coulda been doing today?' Di Maeo asked.

'What?' Levine said.

'I coulda been watching the ball game on television, and I coulda had a big dinner with the family. My sister is in from Scranton, she come all the way in from Scranton 'cause she knows I'm on vacation. So instead I'm talking to a bunch of people who couldn't care less whether a grocer got shot, and who couldn't care at *all* whether a cop caught one.'

Meriwether the hairbag said, 'Now, now, fellows, it's all part of the game, all part of the game.'

In two separate locked rooms down the corridor, Willis was interrogating Sonia Sobolev, and Genero was interrogating Robert Hamling. Neither of the suspects had exercised their right to an attorney. Hamling, who claimed he had nothing to hide, seemed pleased in fact that he could get his story on the record. He repeated essentially what he had told them in the apartment: Lewis Scott had been on a bum acid trip and had thrown himself out the window while Hamling had done all he could to prevent the suicide. The stenographer listened to every word, his fingers moving silently over his machine.

Sonia Sobolev apparently felt no need for an attorney because she did not consider herself mixed up in the death of Lewis Scott. Her version of the story differed greatly from Hamling's. According to Sonia, Hamling had met the bearded Scott that afternoon and the two had banked around the city for a while, enjoying each other's company. Scott was indeed celebrating something – the arrival from home of a two-hundred-dollar money order, which he had cashed and which, in the form of ten-dollar bills, was now nestling in a money belt under his shirt. Hamling had gone back to Scott's apartment with him, and tried to get him drunk. When that failed, he asked Scott if he didn't think they needed a little female company, and when Scott agreed that might not be a bad idea, Hamling had gone downstairs to call Sonia.

'What did he tell you when he met you later?' Willis asked.

'Well, I got off the train,' Sonia said, 'and Bobby was waiting there for me. He said he had this dumb plastic hippie in an apartment near by, and the guy had a money belt with two hundred dollars in it, and Bobby *wanted* that money. He said the only way to get it was to convince the guy to take off his clothes. And the only way to do that was for me to do it first.' Sonia shrugged. 'So we went up there.'

'Yes, what happened then?'

'Well, I went in the john and combed my hair and then I took off my blouse. And I went out to the other room without any blouse on. To see if I could, well, get him excited, you know. So he would take off his clothes. We were all drinking a lot of wine.'

'Were you smoking?'

'Pot, you mean? No.'

'So what happened?'

'Well, he finally went in the john, too, and got undressed. He was wearing blue jeans and a Charlie Brown sweat shirt. And he *did* have a money belt. He was wearing a money belt.'

'Did he take that off, too?'

'Yes.'

'And then what?'

'Well, he came back to the mattress, and we started fooling around a little you know, just touching each other. Actually, I was sort of keeping him busy while Bobby went through the money belt. Trouble is, he *saw* Bobby. And he jumped up and ran to where Bobby was standing with the money belt in his hands, and they started fighting, and that

... that was when Bobby pushed him out the window. We split right away. I just threw on my jacket, and Bobby put on his coat, and we split. I didn't even remember the blouse until much later.'

'Where's the money belt now?' Willis asked.

'In Bobby's apartment. Under his mattress.'

In the other room, Hamling kept insisting that Lewis Scott was an acid freak who had thrown himself out the window to the pavement below. Di Maeo knocked on the door, poked his head inside, and said, 'Dick, you send some suspect dope to the lab?'

'Yeah,' Genero said.

'They just phoned. Said it was oregano.'

'Thanks,' Genero said. He turned again to Hamling. 'The stuff in Lewis Scott's refrigerator was oregano,' he said.

'So what?' Hamling said.

'So tell me one more time about this big acid freak you got involved with.'

In the squad-room outside, Carella sat at his desk typing a report on Goldenthal and Gross. Goldenthal had been taken to Buenavista, the same hospital that was caring for Andy Parker, whom he had shot. Gross had refused to say a word to anyone. He had been booked for Armed Robbery and Murder One, and was being held in one of the detention cells downstairs. Carella looked extremely tired. When the telephone on his desk rang, he stared at it for several moments before answering it.

'Eighty-seventh Squad,' he said, 'Carella.'

'Steve, this is Artie Brown.'

'Hello, Artie,' Carella said.

'I just wrapped up this squeal on North Trinity. Guy came home, and they're happily in the sack.'

'Good for them,' Carella said. 'I wish *I* was happily in the sack.'

'You want me to come back there, or what?'

'What time is it?'

'Seven-thirty.'

'Go home, Artie.'

'You sure? What about the report?'

'I'm typing it now.'

'Okay then, I'll see you,' Brown said.

'Right,' Carella said, and put the receiver back on to its cradle, and looked up at the wall clock, and sighed. The telephone on Carl Kapek's desk was ringing.

'Eighty-seventh,' he said, 'Kapek speaking.'

'This is Danny Gimp,' the voice on the other end said.

'Hello, Danny, what've you got for me?'

'Nothing,' Danny said.

Di Maeo, Meriwether, and Levine were packing it in, hoping to resume their vacations without further interruption. Levine seemed certain that Brown and Carella would get promotions out of this one; there were always promotions when you cracked a case involving somebody doing something to a cop. Di Maeo agreed with him, and commented that some guys had all the luck. They went down the iron-runged steps and past the muster desk, and through the old building's entrance doors. Meriwether stopped on the front steps to tie his shoelace. Alex Delgado was just getting back to the station house. He chatted for only a moment, said goodnight to all of them, and went inside. It was almost seven forty-five, and some of the relieving shift was already in the squad-room.

In a little while, the daywatch could go home.

Kapek had been cruising from bar to bar along The Stem since 8 PM. It was now twenty minutes past eleven, and his heart skipped a beat when the black girl in the red dress came through the doors of Romeo's on Twelfth Street. The girl sashayed past the men sitting on stools along the length of the bar, took a seat at the far end near the telephones, and crossed her legs. Kapek gave her ten minutes to eye every guy in the joint, and then walked past her to the telephones. He dialled the squad-room, and got Finch, the catcher on the relieving team.

'What are you doing?' Finch wanted to know.

'Oh, cruising around,' Kapek said.

'I thought you went home hours ago.'

'No rest for the weary,' Kapek said. 'I'm about to make a bust. If I'm lucky.'

'Need some help?'

'Nope,' Kapek said.

'Then why the hell did you call?'

'Just to make some small talk,' Kapek said.

'I've got a knifing on Ainsley,' Finch answered. 'Go make small talk someplace else.'

Kapek took his advice. He hung up, felt in the coin return chute for his dime, shrugged, and went out to sit next to the girl at the bar.

'I'll bet your name is Suzie,' he said.

'Wrong,' the girl said, and grinned. 'It's Belinda.'

'Belinda, you are one beautiful piece,' Kapek said.

'You think so, huh?'

'I do most sincerely think so,' Kapek said. 'May I offer to buy you a drink?'

'I'd be flattered,' Belinda said.

They chatted for close to twenty minutes. Belinda indicated that she found Kapek highly attractive; it was rare that a girl could just wander into a neighbourhood bar and find someone of Kapek's intelligence and sensitivity, she told him. She indicated, too, that she would like to spend some time with Kapek a little later on, but that her husband was a very jealous man and that she couldn't risk leaving the bar with Kapek because word might get back to her husband and then there would be all kinds of hell to pay. Kapek told her he certainly understood her position. Still, Belinda said, I sure would love to spend some time with you, honey. Kapek nodded.

'What do you suppose we can do?' he asked.

'You can meet me outside, can't you?'

'Sure,' he said. 'Where?'

'Let's drink up. Then I'll leave, and you can follow me out in a few minutes. How does that sound?'

Kapek looked up at the clock behind the bar. It was ten minutes to twelve. 'That sounds fine to me,' he said.

Belinda lifted her whisky sour and drained it. She winked at him and swivelled away from the bar. At the door, she turned, winked again, and then went out. Kapek gave her five minutes. He finished his scotch and soda, paid for the drinks, and went out after her. Belinda was waiting on the next corner. She signalled to him, and began walking rapidly up The Stem. Kapek nodded and followed her. She walked two blocks east, looked back at him once again, and turned abruptly left on Fifteenth Street. Kapek reached the corner and drew his pistol. He hesitated, cleared his throat to let them know he was coming, and then rounded the corner.

A white man was standing there with his fist cocked. Kapek thrust the gun into his face and said, 'Everybody stand still.' Belinda started to break. He grabbed her wrist, flung her against the brick wall of the building, said, 'You, too, honey,' and took his handcuffs from his belt.

He looked at his watch.

It was a minute to midnight.

Another day was about to start.

Ed McBain
Like Love 60p

A young girl jumps to her death, a salesman gets blown apart, and two semi-nude bodies found on a bed, seem to have died in a love pact, Spring was really here for the 87th Precinct . . . Carella and Hawes thought the double suicide stank of homicide, but they couldn't get a break. Fortunately, Hawes had something going with Christine . . . like love.

Doll 60p

A man grasping a kitchen knife slashed relentlessly at lovely Tinka Sachs. Obscenities and blade enveloped her in spittle and blood. In the next room, the child Anna clung fiercely to her doll all night long . . . Carella found himself the prisoner of a lush brunette who would kill a man as easily as she would seduce him.

Axe 60p

January brought a sunless lack of cheer to the 87th Precinct. There would be no happy new year for George Lasser. An axe had split his skull wide open. Then someone killed a cop. It looked like being a lousy month for Detectives Hawes and Carella . . .

Fuzz 80p

With the temperature 12 below zero there was nothing good happening in the 87th Precinct – but for the usual quota of muggings, rapes, knifings and burglaries. And then the city officials began to get killed off one by one . . .

'The best of today's procedural school of police stories – lively, inventive, convincing, suspenseful and wholly satisfactory'.
NEW YORK TIMES

John D. MacDonald
The Deep Blue Goodbye 50p

There was a special kind of hell for men like Junior Allen, and McGee had three good reasons for putting him there – Cathy, Lois and Patty.

The Girl in the Plain Brown Wrapper 60p

'Wholly absorbing suspense . . . intricate plot and additions to the McGee psychologies of relationships between the sexes and, on an entirely different level, between the races' NEW YORK TIMES

The Long Lavender Look 60p

McGee discovers a hidey-hole of pornographic trash, drug capsules and polaroid prints of thirteen nude girls in a town where law and order never changed – only short-changed . . .

Pale Grey for Guilt 60p

'As meaty as usual . . . with lots of expertise on how to slug financial sharks' SUN

A Purple Place for Dying 50p

McGee should have got out of town fast, but he wanted to find out about Mona – and why she got a .44 Magnum bullet punched through her spine . . .

The Dreadful Lemon Sky 60p

Running scared, Carrie Milligan turned up at 3 a.m. with a stack of dollar bills for McGee to guard . . . Two weeks later she turned up again in Florida, on County Road 858, alone and very dead.

Looking for answers, McGee walked into a big right fist and a mess of Jamaican grass, greed, passion and paranoia.

'Includes one of the best descriptions of a fight to the death I've ever read. Thanks McGee' EVENING STANDARD

Peter O'Donnell
Sabre-Tooth 70p

The second caper of Modesty and Willie Garvin takes them on an exotic and danger-filled trail from London to Paris, Lisbon and Tangier, bringing them to the mountains of Hindu Kush – home of a modern Genghis Khan with an army of ruthless mercenaries.

'Fantastic adventure and compelling drama'
HALIFAX EVENING CHRONICLE

Last Day in Limbo 75p

Somebody wanted Modesty Blaise in a big way – big enough to set up a very expensive kidnap operation . . .

'A sharply-twisting story-line, varied locations, a formidable criminal project, lots of healthy violence, nasty villains . . . I was gripped from the start and stayed gripped' KINGSLEY AMIS, EVENING STANDARD